vintage science fiction

BOOKS BY RICHARD E. PECK

FICTION

Schmidt's Mill

Philly Amateurs

Strategy of Terror

Dead Pawn

Something for Joey

NON-FICTION

All the Courses in the Kingdom:
  An American Plays at the Birthplace of Golf

The New Mexico Experience: A Confluence of Cultures

Poems: Nathaniel Hawthorne

COLUMNS

Traveling at My Desk: Stories for 52 Weekends

Passing Through

SCIENCE FICTION

Vintage Science Fiction

Final Solution

> Theodore Sturgeon writes: "Culling the length and breadth of speculative fiction as I do affords a number of peak moments, explosive discoveries. Imagine for the first time finding Delaney, Disch, Lafferty... Well here's another one. Richard E. Peck in Final Solution has written a yarn ... which will curl up your toes in delight. Coupled with a swift, bright narrative style and a coruscating sense of humor is a sharply serious social commentary... dealing with the University.... Mix in a lot of laughter... a fistful of genius for characterization (and caricature) and a fine feel for language and you have a rough idea of Richard Peck's recipe—and clear notice to watch for the name again."
> *Galaxy Bookshelf*

Richard E. Peck

To Alan
Richard E Peck — Luckily not all of these "came true"

vintage
science
fiction

Best wishes

REPertory

REPertory Publishing
Placitas, New Mexico

First REPertory Publishing Edition, 2012
REPertory Publishing
Placitas, NM
www.richardepeck.com

©2012 by Richard E. Peck
All rights reserved
First edition

ISBN 978-0-9838524-3-8 (trade paperback)

1 3 5 7 9   10 8 6 4 2

Printed in the United States of America
Text set in Arno Pro with Boldina display
Design and composition: Barbara Haines

Vintage Science Fiction is a work of fiction. The characters, locations, and events portrayed herein are fictional or are used fictionally.

Dedicated to:

an unregenerate Science Fiction fan, an accomplished aerospace engineer, and NASA's Chief Technologist, my son

MASON PECK

contents

Introduction   ix

In Alien Waters   1969   1

The Guardians   1970   15

A Slight Detour   1971   30

The Man Who Faded Away   1971   48

Commuter Special   1972   57

Ethel Pease   1972   70

Gantlet   1972   75

Deliveryman   1975   91

Heel!   1975   110

Fragments of a Second Friday   1976   130

Sums   with John Jakes, 1976   145

Re-porter   1977   163

Take a Number   1979   169

About the Author   179

introduction

Readers often ask, "Where do you get your ideas?" Here's one feeble answer.

In 1969 at Temple University I embarrassed a few English Dept. colleagues by teaching what I've since been told was the first college "academic credit-earning" Science Fiction class in the country. There were 23 students in the class, most of them SF fans/"fanatics" and therefore more widely read in SF than I. Most of them hoped to write their own SF stories, "soon,"—one of them announced, "When I get a good idea."

As the designated professor, I professed, "The idea isn't the most important. It's the execution of it that counts." An unaccomplished author, I had no trouble being glib.

We made a pact. At the urging of student David Paskow—among the most "fanatic" there—I offered them an idea, and a "task," their homework. Over the weekend each of us would write his or her story; and Monday we'd compare them. I predicted 24 richly different tales spawned by even the silliest basic idea. The silly idea was my contribution.

I blurted out, "Let's say the Titanic didn't hit an iceberg." (I've never known where that came from). "An iceberg hit the Titanic. Now go ye forth and type!"

Monday we piled the results on my desk. It was a small pile. Two twenty-page stories, one by David Paskow, who'd inspired the exercise, and mine. There was an anonymous, aborted four-page start, by the girl who always sat 90 degrees offline, facing the exit. And three single-page undeveloped restatements of the idea, only one of them pornographic. We discussed them all. David took his home to revise. I revised mine that afternoon, stuck it in an envelope, and mailed it to Mercury Press. The other efforts lay on my desk, unclaimed. The next morning I saw the janitor toss them in the trash. Everyone's a critic.

In November, 1969, *Venture* published "In Alien Waters," my first SF story. It was worth more to me that the 3¢ a word it earned.

I offered to submit David's story but he demurred. He wanted to keep working on it. I hope it found its way into the David C. Paskow Science Fiction Collection at Temple University's Paley Library. That fine collection was established far too soon, with David's posthumous contribution of his 5,000-volume SF collection.

The point is, it's hard to say where ideas come from or where they will lead. They exist all around us, and they spring to mind when the need for them arises. I owed an idea to the class. David Paskow mysteriously inspired it . . . and others since.

In a recent phone conversation my son (long an unrecovered SF fan) suggested that I collect my SF stories for re-publication.

"I don't have that many," I told him.

"I'll bet there's 30!"

"No chance!" But, swamped by his exuberance, ignoring the counting error, I pursued his "idea" and gathered a small stack of pulps from dark closet shelves. Twenty-one of them, their bright covers faded or tattered, page corners dog-eared, but most of them fun to re-read and recollect, even 30 to 40 years after their ideas had come to me.

There's no *Analog* entry in the bunch, more *Amazing* and *Fantastic* stories (thank you Ted White) than *Fantasy and Science Fiction*. Collectively, the stories offer a few humanoid aliens (but no Bug Eyed Monsters). Space travel, of course. Dubious science but useful technology (broadcast power, today still in our future, and casual references to a GPS I "invented.") Few "heroes," the protagonists were generally mid-level managers stuck in grim future societies. Fun to write, fun for me to re-read, here they are: 2/3 of my 21 SF stories, not the 30 my son so generously estimated.

Some of them reflect ideas generated for (and BY) that SF class. Others came to me as ideas do—when I needed one. I now recognize that several of them might have combined to become a bleak urban novel I never wrote, a sequel to *Final Solution* (Doubleday, 1972, now on Kindle). Until re-reading them, I had never considered 17 years of commuting on the Media Local—Swarthmore into Philadelphia and back—"inspiring."

I still don't. But the experience offered ideas, and lots of time for reflection. That's all you need.

In Alien Waters

first published in *Venture*, November 1969

Remember it? Not half! Near fifteen hundred dead there was. Women and little tykes crying. And that one body in the water— ugh! After a row like that I'm not likely to forget, am I? I told the inquiry board, but I'm no officer, why believe me? I don't care what that lot say. I know what I saw!

Moments after breaking out of subspace at the end of what should have been the ship's second-last jump, Captain Rosh recognized his dilemma. They had somehow missed their preset coordinates and materialized not in deep space but within the gravitational field of some large body. Still groggy and shaking off the mind-wrenching effects of the jump, he scanned the blurred meters dancing before his eyes. The spectroscope showed him a G-type star. Grav-field-plot indicated the presence of several massive bodies in the system, but Rosh couldn't spare the time to check further, not with one of those bodies looming huge and deadly on his viewer. He shielded his unblinking eyes and reduced the intensity of free-atmosphere light till the planet appeared olive-colored through his opaque filter. He felt his crew regaining consciousness in their separate compartments, but he wouldn't wait.

"Crash imminent!" he drove the thought home into their clouded minds, and then ignored them as he jammed his webbed hands onto the panel sensors and linked himself to the ship's damage control units. The trouble was obvious—a leak in the aft external bulkhead, crisis dimension. Already their precious water scattered behind the ship in a stream of sparkling frozen crystals, dotting a glistening arc which pointed toward their probable deaths on the planet every moment growing larger beneath them.

He pressed the sealant dispersal stud and simultaneously double-locked the watertight iris-hatch which isolated the after compartment, wasting an instant on the luxury of a quick apology to Sisson, the engineering officer now floating in the cramped space that would soon become his arid tomb. Then he paused, a moment's delay obvious to the suddenly alert crew who lay in disciplined silence, awaiting orders.

"Sealant ineffectual. Go to maximum refrigeration."

The crew responded by joining the force of their anxious minds, driving the refrigeration unit to its extreme and freeing Rosh to concentrate on slowing the ship's descent. Rime ice sparkled on the huge ship's hull and thickened, redoubling its depth with agonizing slowness.

Still Rosh's dilemma compounded itself. He fought to slow their descent enough not to exceed the freezing powers of the scout-ship's equipment while he calculated optimum safe entry speed. Too rapid an entry would melt the accumulating crust of ice on the outer bulk heads faster than even his handpicked crew could urge the equipment to replace it. And yet too slow a descent would mark them as a target for whatever life-form dominated the planet now swelling gigantic in his viewer. He didn't *know* that a reception committee would prove antagonistic, but caution made him assume the worst.

He lost contact with Sisson and felt the tension build in the minds of the other two crew members. Hysor, his second-in-command floating in the bow hold, Myrsha the ship's linguist and cultural expert at her station in the third of the ship's watertight compartments. He shared the mood "reassurance" with them, but they had already conquered momentary sadness at the loss of one-fourth of their pooled sentience.

Rosh watched the planet surface swimming closer in his viewer. The edge of the terminator on the cloud-dotted mass below bisected an ocean. Though he couldn't risk the lateral movement necessary to reach full darkness, he could guide the ship into the dusky band of twilight where darkness would soon cover and protect them. Their chanced for survival increased by the second.

He shared "pleasure." Moments before he had masked his fears—no one captained a Cyran scout-ship without that ability, so rare among his youthful subordinates. On emerging from subspace he had immediately suppressed the thought that the planet now clutching his crippled ship in the tug of its awesome gravity might have been burned out, somehow waterless and therefore a deathtrap. But his view of the cloud cover had dispelled that fear, and the ocean loomed larger and more hospitable as they neared it.

"Captain why did . . . ?"

"OUT!" Rosh slammed his anger through the ship, punishing the questioner with "indecisive meddling!" He knew Myrsha shriveled, embarrassed within herself at the comment, but his was no time for niceties. He concentrated instead on their descent. The atmosphere was even thicker than he had imagined, an almost incredible blanket of noxious gasses surrounding this world.

He slowed the ship again, lifting and flattening its arc to head toward the polar region and more hospitably cold waters where the rime ice building ever thicker on the ship's surface might endure without constant attention. The ship seemed to hesitate above the gray-green swells; then her 20,000 tons plunged safely beneath the waves.

Rosh leveled her vertical in the water, the tri-pronged bow a full hundred meters into the sub-surface darkness. He reduced opacity on the viewers and kicked back from the control panel to center himself in the compartment. He rotated lazily and let his eyes sweep over the belt of viewers mounted in the bulkhead, checking the full three-hundred-sixty degrees around them. All clear.

It was fair cold topside, for them as was there to notice. Now me, I was off-shift and had done with some port the wife sent along in me kit, so I takes me a constitutional on deck. It was by way of what you might call a celebration. Here was I, a promotion and a new ship. Not that I didn't deserve it, mind you. Four years an oiler, I was, before the company seen fit to do me proper.

"Report."

"Refrigeration holds," Hysor responded. "Maximum output no longer necessary. Sea water tests approximately three percent saline materials in solution."

"Habitable environment. Detectors indicate no fully conscious organisms, our immediate surroundings," followed Myrsha's analysis.

At least she hadn't let his reprimand divert her from her duties. "Good girl, "he flashed back, basking then in the satisfied glow she shared with him and Hysor. "Sealant unnecessary for the moment," Rosh continued. "The ice cover blocks the leak effectively. But we'll have to maintain the surface crust till we can work out a way of mending the sprung seam."

"Captain?" It was Myrsha again. "Water temperature at freeze-point and cooling. May one suggest semi-permanent crust?"

"Agreed. Conform to vessel's contours. A five-meter layer ought to conceal us as well. If . . . make it ten." He sensed a muted buzz of consciousness. "Sisson?"

"Here, Captain."

"Good to have you back. Anything serious?"

"Brief hyperventilation. No apparent loss of faculties. Just a little dizzy, now."

"Stay with the external temperature control. Opaque the ice except over sensory equipment."

"Aye, sir."

"We'll open the hatch where we're sure it's safe. What's the water level in your compartment?"

"Gill-high, I'd guess. The leak caught me by surprise, water dropped a full meter before I spotted the loss, but I'm lying safely below the surface now."

"Stand by." One pull of his powerful arms and Rosh reached the control panel once more where he tied himself to the ship's sensors and sought the error that had caused them to mis-jump so badly. But the preset coordinates dissolved in a chaotic whirl. Only the last jump lay recorded in the computer's automatic memory bank. At least that fail-safe had functioned properly. But the other evidence was undeniable: the computer had failed.

Quickly he buried the thought, simultaneously accepting it as fact and recognizing the impossibility of believing it. To clear away the confusion, he let training take over. "Review all data," he reminded himself, again holding the thought below the verge of consciousness and away from the crew, who withdrew into themselves and maintained silence in recognition of the captain's need for isolation.

Subspace drive is infallible. No scout-ship computer ever fails. Both facts are axiomatic. Still, when evidence indicates to the contrary, a capable mind discards axioms. Rosh was a captain at nine years old only because he could adapt. Most of the scout-ships were headed by middle-aged men already approaching their teens. He hadn't reached his eminence by being stupid, and therefore accepted with only the slightest qualm what evidence taught.

That must have been the same feeling, he reassured himself, when the first scout-ship brought back its terrifying news only twenty annuals before—the report that on some planets a surface life-form had actually achieved dominance. No one had believed it; the very thought that intelligence could develop in such inimical surroundings was laughable. Until a second ship had verified the report. By then it was too late. The Committee had already executed the first crew for deviation and "withholding," floating them to the surface of Cyra's Grand Ocean to die the painful death of gas immersion.

Rosh held back a shudder at the thought. He reviewed his orders to calm himself. Five maximum jumps, the last two exceeding the limits of his charts. Seek out other tool-using life-forms. Observe but make no contact. Return all data to The Committee.

He was prepared to find a surface life-form—though no ships in his lifetime had—his training saw to that. But the concept of a dominant one still lay outside the range of his full comprehension. The Committee called it a fact, so of course he believed—intellectually—but could place no more emotional credence in it than in the ichthyologists' myth that man might have adapted from a pre-historic surface organism into his present evolutionary stage. It smacked of fantasy, like the widespread speculation among Cyran scientists that such a life-form might be sub-psychic, might communicate by vocal sounds or pantomime like the simplest Cyran crustacean. He couldn't imagine such isolation, such lack of oneness with the race.

The band sounded like a summer Saturday on the big pier at Brighton, everyone singing and laughing. It's a grand, gay time, a maiden voyage like that. But mainly in First Class—not below decks, them with their long faces, and foreigners all to a man.

Rosh snorted his disbelief. In his three previous expeditions—admittedly all within the confine of the charted universe—he had come upon no life-form more aberrant than a microscopic organism on Feld-two which seemed able to survive out of water for several minutes. And that minor feat Cyrans had long ago mastered with the aid of an aqua-lung, a self-contained and recycled water supply which drew minute quantities of free oxygen from the mass of poisonous gases blanketing the surface of any planet with which he was familiar.

With which *all* Cyrans were familiar, he recognized. "What one knows, all know"—an axiom taught him at the instant of his preconscious emergence from the egg. Only The Committee might withhold knowledge. And perhaps a scout-ship captain, for a brief time, under direct orders from The Committee. But that time had passed.

"Here is our situation," Rosh summarized. "Subspace plot was in error for the last jump." He paused a moment as disbelief welled up around him in the other three minds attuned to his. "I *know*," he emphasized.

"We know," came reluctant acquiescence.

"The loss of fluid and consequent imbalance may have caused it. Immaterial. But we can't maintain surface ice crust in subspace. Any jump without it opens us up to a probable repetition of out current problem. One solution: repair the damaged bulkhead, then try to jump back."

"Navigation?" came the question from Hysor.

"Last jump still recorded in the memory bank. We can return that far, then resort to normal drive via the charts, unless we can also repair the computer at that time."

"But normal drive..."

"Yes, Myrsha. We'll all be dead long before the ship gets home. But once started, it should pass near enough to be reclaimed. And there is a chance we can make the necessary repairs, once we locate ourselves on the charts and recalibrate the equipment.— Sisson? Verify."

"Agreed, Captain. A chance."

Rosh knew they felt the hesitation in the engineer's thought, but he couldn't prevent that. They were better off knowing the truth about their plight. He probed gently for signs of excessive fear, for potential imbalance in his crew, but found nothing serious enough to disturb him. Only a strange, half-formed twinkle from Myrsha felt out of place—something about "not all dead," yet more feeling than a thought, and not clear enough to restate.

"Mysha?"

"Sorry, Captain. Ready."

"Better. Hysor join with Sisson and effect repairs. We've lost approximately two percent of our water. We could destroy the surface crust and take on more water through the leak itself, but it's not worth the delay. Better to contract the hull plates to conform. Our jump will be delicate enough with a full ship. I don't want any interior turbulence to contend with."

"Aye, sir."

"While we're here, Myrsha and I will conduct whatever survey we can. We may as well collect all possible data before leaving."

And that lot in the boiler room! To listen to them you'd think not a one knew his place, bandying about the passengers' first names like your common poor relations. "Isn't Cosmo the toff?" says one of them potato-munchers to me, bold as brass. Meaning Sir Cosmo Duff-Gordon, don't you know.

Rosh concentrated on mapping the topography of the ocean floor beneath them, Myrsha on cataloguing life-forms within reach of their sensing gear. The survey would be incomplete, but however skimpy it would please The Committee more than their returning empty-handed. As they worked individually, they shared their findings, including in the pool of their merged consciousness a touch of their occupied friends who now concentrated their main energies of the task of repairing the sprung seam. Should any of the four—each in his own sealed compartment—survive the trip back, he would possess the combined knowledge of all, making possible a full report to The Committee. Their individual lives were of little importance in the span of history; the race would go on, accumulating data, analyzing it, progressing, developing. The past taught them that, the future would be no different.

With an unoccupied part of his "self," Rosh hymned the past as an exercise in discipline. Only through joint effort had they come so far. And so they would plunge on. Consider the man who had first steeled himself to break the surface tension of the Grand Ocean and lunge upward into the blinding light and lung-searing atmosphere. His suicide, instantaneously shared by all Cyrans, had taught them the beginnings of their destiny.

Then came the aqualung. And the first telescope raised to exist half in the safety of the sea and half probing the upper gases air like a challenge thrust up toward the stars. All part of a pattern, indomitable will and determination, the questing spirit that made man master his environment. That accomplished, then to leave it all behind, courageously to venture forth in self-contained microcosms of the sea itself, seeking new worlds. But seeking not to conquer, only to comprehend. So long as an unanswered question remained, man was not man, but nearly more than the anglerfish, a creature of contrivance and appetite.

We was ripping off twenty, maybe twenty-two knots, just flying. And chill in the air to frost your very bones. But all the while I could hear them three lovely screws just singing away under us.

"Rosh! Feel it?" Mysha demanded.

For moments he had sensed a strange tremor, unidentifiable and therefore important. "What do you make it?"

"It's—excuse me—it's *almost* sentience. Sorry if I can't put it any better."

"Sisson?"

"No, sir. Out of reach. But it's different. All around us there are organisms capable of repeating learned behavior, but not creating. Yet this is different. Almost intelligence, if... I really can't say, Captain."

"In the surrounding ice?"

Myrsha thought denial. "They're all natural floes, some nearly our size, but totally lifeless. I checked on that earlier."

So had he—as she must have known—but he covered the thought. She had begun to act somehow "separate," as if she were withholding, an idea he dismissed as unworthy. "It will explain itself," he told her. "Nothing to worry about. But thanks for the comments."

She shared "pleasure" and returned to her survey while Rosh completed mapping the area within reach of his scanners. Then a thought struck. "Myrsha? Could it be some sort of apparatus? Equipment?"

She denied it. "Not possible without accompanying signs of intelligence, but I do know why you feel that. It's a combination of the two, senseless as that sounds."

"We'll see."

"Repairs completed. Captain," Sisson reported. "No difficulty with the leak. Do we check the computers now, or...?"

"Wait. I know we can reverse the last jump without error. But resetting the computers might cost us that apparent certainty. Let's wait till we're nearer home. Then we'll..."

"Rosh! That tremor again," Mysha interrupted.

The captain probed the immediate vicinity but found nothing. "I don't spot it. But we're ready to go. Let's not risk anything unforeseen. The Committee can analyze our sensations and the instrument recordings. They many be able to account for it. Stand by for buoyancy."

He released the depth stabilizers and checked the instruments quickly as the ship lifted silently toward the surface. Through his concentration, perhaps because he now ignored the difference he had recently noticed in Myrsha, momentary insight told him that her time was approaching—she would spawn soon.

"Yes, Rosh," she interrupted. "Get us *all* home, will you?" and then was silent.

The four shared "delight" and returned to concentrating on lift-out. The ship broke the surface and her bow lunged suddenly into the midnight air. Rosh focused on stability and prepared once more to commit his ship and crew to the supra-surface dangers lying between them and home, the Grand Ocean.

I was leaning out watching the phosphorus splashing back off the bow, when I look up and there it is. Not half sudden! Straight out of nowhere like a bloody great mountain.

Rosh dove deeper into his thoughts. His attention blanked out everything but the task at hand, feeling himself one with the entire ship as she hung poised, half in, half out of the water. "Cut refrigeration. We'll burn away the crust as we lift." But then the strange tremor returned, stronger now, and he was still unable to define or locate its source. Irritated at even so slight an impotence in himself, he scanned the depths beneath them for a final instant before lifting.

We swerve at the last minute and scrape along the berg, so close I could near touch it. Great chunks clattered all over the deck when we hit her. But you just ask Fleet. He was on lookout and saw it all. Or Mr. Murdoch, as was on the bridge when we hit.

"COLLISION! COLLISION! A VESSEL!" his crew's combined thoughts pierced the shield of his concentration as he felt the ship heel wildly over on her side, thrown off line. The shock hurled them into a tight, spinning arc. Instruments blurred before him, and he snatched his hands free from the pain of the damage-control sensors now throbbing their news of the ship's destruction—the bow was shattered, burst open in the deadly air above, scattering ice and debris in a resounding cascade back over the ship.

A searing pain told them of Hysor, his violent exposure to the atmosphere, and then the merciful death as the force of the collision itself crushed the life from his gasping body.

Power faded.

"SURVIVAL!" Rosh ordered, and blew the exterior hatches to free himself and the other two for their desperate dive into the unfamiliar ocean surrounding them.

"Unsinkable," they called her—huh! A bare two hours later I watched her founder by the head. That's when I seen the body. There am I, treading water in all this wreckage, deck chairs and what you will, just waiting for one of the collapsible boats to pick me up. A corpse floats past, all torn and mangled, but I swear it—webbed hands, no hair at all and these layers of slits tight

In Alien Waters 13

here by the collarbone. Gills they was. And him stone naked. I fair blushed to see it.

They would survive, Rosh knew. Unknown, uncharted, rife with dangers unforeseen and unpredictable, the ocean still held out its conforming depths to them. More than merely "they," the race would survive.

"Yes, Rosh, came Myrsha's anguished thought. "But here? In alien waters? Our children…

"The race will survive. I know."

"We know."

In the murky depths he finally located Sisson and Myrsha. Together they dove safely clear of the gigantic hulk drifting slowly past them toward the black ocean floor.

Believe it or not, it's all one to me. I know what I know. There's things about in the deep waters as are better left alone. So when you're done with the questions, it's inland I'm headed, to open a tobacconist's, or a sweet shop, with not an ocean in sight. And it's a punch-up for the first man as much as names the Titanic to me.

The Guardians

first published in *If Science Fiction*, September–October 1970

While sounds of the anniversary celebration wafted softly from the dark valley below, George Harmon scrambled over the crest of the ridge and cowered beside a huge boulder, gasping for breath. Scraps of shale bit into his knees and he cursed the darkness he himself had chosen for protection. Both moons lay low on the horizon of the summer sky, the nearer a mere crescent, the farther nearly full but dim in the distance. A perfect night for the test he had planned. Yet even as his eyes plumbed the darkness he sensed the shadow circling overhead. Shrinking against the lichen-crusted rocks, he waited.

The shadow came again, blotting out a patch of brilliant stars which flickered rampant in their jet background—a milk white blur soared above him in lazy circles.

Harmon took his bearings from the boulder and pointed himself down the far side of the ridge toward a cave mouth he had spotted during one of his solitary walks only days before, a sanctuary. If he could reach that cave unseen, his pursuer might—for one instant—lose track of him, might become separated, George would finally sever the indefinable bond that united them. He felt little real hope but it was a chance.

Seizing a large stone in one hand, he lurched to his feet and crashed through brush that raked his face, tore at his clothes with brittle fingers, scraping and clutching at him. Heavy wings fluttered overhead, but the pulsing sound only drove him faster.

The cave mouth gaped its welcome, a bit of the night sky planted darkling here among the rocks, and Harmon sprawled inside, simultaneously hurling the stone in his hand down the talus slope ahead of him. Bounding racket clattered away through the rocks, a false trail to mislead his pursuer. Then he lay panting and waited.

He swallowed nothing as the cotton in his mouth dissolved and his heaving chest slowed. Acrid sweat stung his eyes. All was quiet except for muted snatches of song drifting through the still night from the celebration he had left behind. That, too, was part of his plan: caught up in the excitement of the evening, the guardians might not notice his absence. A foolish hope, perhaps, but his only one.

After a long moment he risked a quick glance outside.

His guardian perched some ten yards from him, preening and white, waiting with maddening faithfulness for Harmon to emerge from the cave. Anger swelled in him, drowned at once in the wave of peace that came unbidden to wash over and surround him. He tried to fight the calming aura that bathed his every thought. It was useless. There was no escape.

Harmon rose once more to his feet and, resigned, turned back toward the valley. A draft of cooling night air fanned his neck as the guardian launched itself and swooped low over his bowed head, then winged its way aloft to resume a silent perch on the wind.

Harmon skirted the communal party on the way back to his pneumodome. The detour added thirty minutes to his trip home but he had no wish to meet any of the other colonists now, not with his guardian gleaming aberrant white in the night sky above him like a contemning signpost. He knew that none of the others would admit how radically his guardian's appearance had changed—he could not say whether they showed some mistaken sense of understanding or preferred blindness, but that didn't matter. He knew his guardian—at least by sight. It had changed.

Once the guardian plummeted low across his path to snatch up an adder that lay in deadly ambush. Harmon pointedly ignored the service. He was long past the point of caring, certainly of thanking a creature whose every attention he detested.

His wife sat before their pneumodome, waiting. "George? Where were you? Your clothes! What happened?"

He strode in past her. He knew, without bothering to glance behind him, that the guardian glided gently down to settle on the dome spire and wait with loving concern. During his first few months here he had several times tried to sneak away early in the pre-dawn darkness but the guardian was always alert and waiting. There was no escape.

"George? I asked if you're all right." Marian followed him inside. "I thought you might be sick when you left the party early."

He ignored her and devoted himself to the ritual of checking the compressor whose air flow kept their home erect. It was only through minor, habitual tasks like these that he was able to ignore her irritating solicitude.

"Well? Are you?"

"Who's ever sick here?" he demanded. "And if you give me any of that 'praise guardians crap,' I swear I'll walk out again." He flopped angrily into one of the two clumsy wooden chairs which, with a small table and inflated mattress, comprised the furniture in their temporary quarters. The steady thrum of the compressor drowned out the night noises outside and soothed him in spite of himself.

"You should have stayed. After the dancing we voted to rename the colony. Eden. Isn't that beautiful? John Martin thought of it."

"Eden," George snorted. "I could have guessed. Leave it to our good Captain Martin to come up with that kind of maudlin mindlessness."

Marian merely smiled and reached back to stroke the black feathered head of her guardian, perched docile on the back of her chair. "Pretty bird," she murmured. "Poor George isn't himself tonight."

"Damn it! Don't excuse me to one of them. And haven't I told you to leave that thing outside?"

"Sorry dear." She nodded and her guardian fluttered softly through the susurring air current at the door and out into the night. "But he's so small. He's not really in the way."

"That's just like you, throwing its size up to me. You wander around with a black budgie or whatever following you, while I'm stuck with that reeking albino vulture out there. And don't say you didn't notice it turn color."

"It's really prettier than the others, don't you think?"

"But why do *I* get it?"

"Guardians assign themselves," Marian recited her catechism.

George grunted in irritation and turned away to ignore what he couldn't refute. That fact that no one chose his guardian but was instead chosen had long since become apparent. Perhaps that was what irritated him most, his inability to change what everyone else in the colony had accepted as some sort of foreordained natural fact. Mere hours after their ship had landed, each colonist had found himself the object of special attention lavished on him by a guardian, not chosen but acquired.

One year ago to the day. One year ago they had thundered to a turf-searing landing in the broad valley stretching away to the south from the huge clearing that now contained the pneumodome village and the rich tilled fields that fed the colony. Advance scouting reports had promised them a potential paradise. Rotating on an axis parallel to that of its sun, their new world experienced only mild seasonal changes here in the temperate belt. Except for a twenty-eight-hour day and a four-hundred-day year, the colonists' new home seemed an improved replica of the overpopulated, underfed, war-ridden Earth they had all fled and left.

How far behind, none of them could say. The psychologists all thought it best if they cut the cord completely and started fresh here. Some day their developing technology would let them reestablish contact with other men, wherever their kind would be by then. For now, for the colonists, Eden was meant to be all there was.

The trip outbound from Earth had passed between sleeping and waking—long years in suspended animation. During that time the starvation and skirmishing warfare on Earth had probably increased. The colonists awoke only when the ship's preset equipment sensed "destination." They awoke to new hope, to the sight of a green luxuriant world waiting to welcome them. Even George Harmon had felt, for a brief moment, not his usual cynicism but a twinge of pleasure.

It soon passed. Captain Martin took command and restored Harmon's sense of irritation with his place in the new scheme. "Families to my left, single men over here," Martin ordered. "I want sentries posted till we can inflate the first dormitory and establish security. Then we'll worry about making contact with those birds we've been hearing about."

A snicker ripped through the nervous crowd. Of the facts known to the colonists about their new home, one stood out as the most unlikely: in spite of the planet's hospitable environment, no complex organism had developed sufficiently to dominate the animal life present. Atop the food chain was a single species of birds that traveled in large flocks. The only social organization—but not real intelligence—a sort of silent, empathetic bond. Scouting reports described the birds as small, apparently harmless. The roboprobe scout-ships had brought back to Earth hours of A-V, carefully recorded data—everything, in fact, except the intangibles which only a human survey crew might have noticed. But human crews were unthinkable aboard scout-ships, given the duration of the journey each covered and the massive G-loads which would reduce a frail organism to jelly but troubled the automated equipment not at all. No, the probes had brought back enough data, even about the birds.

And so, during their indoctrination at Colony Central in Utah-state, the potential colonists had of course joked with one another about the hosts who awaited them in their new home. For the entire two months of their training, they had treated one another to puns about "birds of a feather," about their being the "early birds" bound to get the worm, and whatever other strained cleverness occurred to people bone-tired from days of endless psychological screening, adaptability tests and lectures on the problems of founding an agrarian society.

Harmon had avoided the horseplay—birdplay, Marian said once, only to cringe under the withering look her husband had thrown her. He had concentrated instead on satisfying the examiners, all of whom had seemed determined to dissuade him from emigrating, even though his number had come up in the monthly New Life Lottery. Besides the pap they kept muttering about his potential instability, there was the question of his occupation. In theory a legislator like Harmon, a man accustomed to guiding an organized society, should be valuable in any new colony. In practice farmers and laborers proved more effective and reliable. But George had managed to pass all their tests, more often than not masking his true feelings to answer their childishly transparent questions as he knew they expected of a "good risk." That much he could do—anything to escape the terrors of a poisoned atmosphere, of insecticide-laden milk and seawater, of the burgeoning sterility that threatened all who remained on the dying Earth.

So he and Marian had joined the other lucky ones, the groups of three hundred people who fled Earth each month to sink a new foothold for man in some distant corner of the expanding universe.

They had stood with the others while John Martin, elected captain before their liftoff from Earth, apportioned land and set them to work in teams to cannibalize the ship itself for its usable equipment. With the others in the sweating crowd they cheered when the first pneumodome bulged and wobbled erect. And with the others they tensed at the sight of hundred of birds boiling over the horizon to approach and circle the band of wary colonists.

But at first nothing happened.

The birds merely circled, until the colonists separated, each couple or work team to go its own way. Then a strange symbiosis developed between them and the birds—"guardians" they were soon called. Each colonist found himself possessing, or being possessed by, one of the delicate, aromatic gray doves. Not that any formal bond was ever made. Nor was communication between them possible. But a relationship developed nevertheless. A single bird followed each man and each woman night and day, always in sight.

A sentry walking the perimeter of the camp first described the relationship. "I was taking a shortcut through the brush over there and accidentally kicked a hornet's nest. Anyway, they looked like what I'd call hornets. They came buzzing out fit to eat me alive. This bird I'd been seeing behind me all along comes swooping down and gobbles them up so fast I almost couldn't see him work. Not one of them got close enough to sting me. First thing you know, the bird's back, flying in circles over my head. There he is. There."

His report drew echoes from the others in the communal assembly, tales of unexpected aid. The birds, some said, had saved them from snakes writhing through the underbrush. Or the birds had chattered warnings to those few who had thought to eat what appeared to be an apple, a fruit soon proven to be deadly poison. Though no one understood how it worked, everyone was certain it did—the birds knew what threatened man and they protected him.

"Asking nothing in return," Martin had told them. "As far as we know, theirs is honest altruism. You've noticed that it's always the same bird trailing you, right?"

The crowd nodded assent.

"All I can say is, they're some kind of guardians."

"Nonsense!" Harmon shouted. "They must get something out of it. It's not right otherwise. In a symbiosis both partners benefit."

"Then call it parasitism, if you want, with us the parasites," Martin said.

"I still say it's suspicious. And who did they follow around before we got here? Gophers? I say—"

The others booed George down.

Within a week the relationship had become an accepted part of their new life. No one would suffer the least slight uttered about the guardians. One young boy found himself censured for resurrecting a meaningless but apparently clever greeting he had once heard back on Earth: "How's your bird?" His father slapped him—or began to. But he hesitated and the blow didn't land.

Nevertheless, the boy felt reprimanded.

And John Martin's designation stuck. "Guardians" the birds became.

"George?" Marian nudged him gently. "What's wrong?"

He rolled to face her. "You gossip with the others. They tell you stuff. Did anyone ever escape his guardian? Or see one die? And the dogs—they whine any time a guardian gets near. Or they used to."

"Why? They're all—"

"Skip it. Let it go. I should have known better than to ask you. Of course you're content. And the others, not a brain in their heads. Your friend Martin's as stupid as those sheep he coddles all day. But *someone* must recognize how we depend on them. It's not right. It's—it's inhuman."

"We've been all through this, George, a hundred times. I thought John Martin had settled it. The crops prosper, our flocks increase, there hasn't been a quarrel—much less a fight—in the whole year we've been here. If the guardians do any more than we see, it's only to help. I admit I won't go as far as the people who almost worship them, but I can see anything wrong."

"I'll tell you what's wrong. They're getting something from us. They *must* be. Did you ever know anyone to do all the things they do and not expect to get paid? On Earth we—"

Marian smiled. "We're not on Earth, dear."

"So? At least there a man's worth was recognized. Here we're all dirt-grubbing farmers, all except the high muckety-muck Martin. Our leader. He even stinks like his sheep."

"Please. Try to sleep. I'm sure you're worried about nothing." She kissed his cheek and turned away.

Patronizing—just like Martin. Neither of them sense enough to see the obvious.

But he had seen. The feathered parasite that followed his every step had changed radically. In the beginning they were all the same—mourning doves, he might have called them on Earth, gray and delicate, small-boned, graceful, a delight to watch circling in the sunlight as men worked the fields or urged their flocks upslope to the high pasture lands. They seemed to exude an indefinable scent—vaguely pleasant, like freshly laundered linen.

But then changes began to appear in the birds. Marian's guardian, for instance was smaller now. Harmon was sure of it. Smaller and darker, nearly black, as if some evil had worked its transformation on the bird. Harmon's own had grown gigantic, almost as large as an eagle and was turning whiter by the day. He swore he had seen it pass through shades of lighter and lighter gray: leaden, ashen, pearl. Only a few days earlier he had glanced up to see it haunting him, as he walked home from the fields. On impulse he had hurled his hoe at the creature, and it flashed brilliant white in the twilight. Then the brilliance faded. As a single occurrence, the sight might have been blamed on some trick of the fading sunlight, but Harmon refused to accept the notion. He had seen the same phenomenon too often. The creature was whiter: now cream; then milk. He knew. Others must have seen it.

He had even swallowed his dislike for Martin long enough to ask whether anyone had made contact with the guardians, had discovered some way of communicating with them. So many questions unanswered. *Why* did they follow the colonists? And why particular ones? Could a man trade guardians with someone else? But Martin—busy in preparation for the anniversary celebration—had ignored him. And the others, including those few who seemed to fear the guardians, however slightly, refused to understand his questions; they even denied the calming aroma that to followed the guardians everywhere.

It was then that Harmon had decided that he would escape his guardian, kill it if necessary. Settle things once and for all, find out what all this meant.

Tonight, with the community gathered to celebrate a year of peace and plenty, he had gone off alone to make his final test. When that proved fruitless—he sucked a scrape on his forearm and savored the memory of the pain he had felt hurtling through the brush in his futile attempt to escape—when that proved fruitless, he had known what he must do. He smiled his hatred toward the dark dome overhead and toward the bird he knew sat waiting. He would kill his guardian but in such a way that no one else would understand his intention—make the act appear spontaneous, perhaps accidental.

Harmon fell asleep smiling.

For the next few days he only watched. The crops had been harvested, a second planting was already underway. While the work teams sweated and labored at their appointed tasks, Harmon questioned those around him. He soon discovered a pattern: the guardians maintained their distance, usually separated a full twenty to thirty yards from the host to which each had attached itself, unless motioned nearer by the man himself. But in moments of stress, when tempers flared or danger threatrened, they dove nearer. And they brought with them peace—an intangible aura of well-being—almost as though each guardian somehow broadcast placidity and emotional calm. The sentimentalists among Harmon's coworkers called it love, to his disgust.

To test his newly formed theory, Harmon tried provoking arguments. He jostled men working their way down the bean rows; he tripped a boy intentionally. Tempers flared, but nothing more ever came of it. In every case even a hint of anger or distrust drew the guardians nearer and the mood passed. Simultaneously the guardians paled, became for a brief moment lighter in color than they had been.

It was clear. The birds flourished on tension, on hate and fear and anger, on the swelling emotions alien to this world and unknown before man's arrival. Perhaps, Harmon theorized, a man's very body chemistry, imbalanced however slightly in moments of stress, attracted the hypersensitive guardians. As an addict might pay for narcotics, the birds returned a sense of peace and well-being for the emotions they absorbed.

That possibility even accounted for the lack of illness among the colonists, he decided. Injuries were of course rare, with guardians always present to warn of impending danger. But illness was equally rare. In some unexplained way the guardians ministered to their hosts, absorbing or drawing off flashes of anger or unpleasant physical sensations. Though many colonists feared their guardians, everyone seemed content, at peace with himself and his neighbors. Everyone but George Harmon, whose fear of the birds had become loathing. He hated his guardian more by the moment. It grew and paled noticeably, bathing George in the fragrant warmth of affection that only increased his hatred.

Why can't you accept things?" Marian pleaded. "Sometimes I think you're sorry we came to Eden. We're all so happy. John says that if—"

"Martin again!" George slammed his wooden cup against the wall and stared in frustration as it bounced to the floor undamaged. He felt his veins throbbing in his forehead and reached for something to break or tear, but there was nothing. "If you mention him to me once—" He stopped at the sound of heavy wings at the curtain of his dome.

And then he knew. The strongest surge of emotion he had felt in weeks had drawn the creature toward him, like prey to a baited trap.

Martin was that bait. Himself!

Harmon fought the pacific calm that filled the pneumo-dome, and plotted his next move. It would all be so simple.

In the morning he joined the procession moving toward the beanfield they were planting. He followed the planting team down the rows, dragging moist soil over each newly seeded hill with his hoe blade. While he worked, he waited.

Shadows drifted along the tilled rows. The guardians circling overhead. Banter passed among the men, gossip about a new baby born the day before and already under the protection of a guardian.

And then Harmon's moment arrived. John Martin strode toward the workers.

"Martin! I want to see you!"

A few of the other looked curious at his tone but returned to their labors. Only the guardians overhead showed agitation.

"What is it, George?"

Harmon savored the aroma Martin carried, the ripe scent of his flocks. He let a thought blossom full and rich in his mind: *Kill him! Kill him!* The hate swelled and burned with a fiery delight. He watched Martin's gray guardian swoop low in chittering protest and dash itself against Martin's chest; but Martin only paused in bewilderment.

Harmon raised his hoe and lunged at Martin. Fluttering wings grazed his head as his own screeching guardian circled lower. The trap sprung, George whirled. His hoe flashed through the sunlight to chop at the mass of snowy feathers. The hoe swung and struck in frantic, staggered rhythm. A mist of gas and splattering gray droplets spewed from the bird's ruptured breast to shower over Harmon. He sagged suddenly in rapture and reached up outstretched arms to the white feathers drifting gently down through the cloud that permeated his swelling flesh. Then he *knew* and became one with the guardian's fetid intensity. His lungs strained to bursting as he sucked in understanding from the sunlit, rainbow-streaked air.

Plaintive gull cries filled the air. The guardians dove to surround the men who stood rooted in fear at the sight of Harmon writhing on the ground in an agony of joy, bloating and swelling like a maddened cancer. A musky glow of peace and contentment laved over the watchers, tears filling their eyes to blind them.

When they saw once more, they stared bewildered at the shattered guardian, the burden of hate now lifted from its slender frame and returned to its source—that source of mass corruption melting to fuse with the earth.

Sadly they covered the foulness at their feet and returned to work.

Soon no one in Eden remember George Harmon, though on still summer evenings the guardians often swoop low over a single spot of sterility lying barren in the fertile soil.

A Slight Detour

first published in *If Science Fiction*, January–February 1971

Radnor felt a powerful urge to sleep. No reason not to. The prisoner was securely bound. Sleep for a few moments. What would it matter? Sleep, and dream of homecoming. He had earned it. A short nap. Lovely sleep. Quiet and peaceful. Quiet and sleepy. Quiet...

No!

He bolted erect and scrubbed the back of his hand across sagging eyelids, trying to fight the languor that melted inside him. He stumbled and grabbed the command cot stanchions to steady himself. His blurred vision cleared as he shook off his torpor and scanned the cramped cabin . . . and understood. Sitting behind the plasticene psi-shield, his prisoner, Kern, smiled sardonically and raised his eyebrows.

"Nice try," Radnor said. "But not this time."

He shivered inwardly and felt much less confident than he tried to appear. What power Kern must possess! He had entered Radnor's mind, nearly hypnotizing him without even gaining his conscious attention—and through a psi-shield at that. But Radnor hadn't made First Bailiff by being careless, or weak, or easily deceived. Complete this assignment successfully and he would get his final promotion to Division Chief. No more lonely transport trips from Melan's correction block to the psi-test asteroid in its isolated corner of the galaxy.

Be cautious, he told himself. *Kern is special . . .*

But then, so was Radnor. No one in the Bailiff Corps tested so high in survival potential; few had the danger instinct he possessed, a touch of undefined psi that had made him the logical choice as Kern's transport guard. If anyone was a logical choice.

Even the medicos on Melan were unable to define the extent of Kern's abilities. He was unusual—that much they knew—perhaps even unique. More precise definition could wait until the specialists took over when Radnor dropped him at the psi-test center (*when*—he refused to think *if*).

He had studied Kern's scanty dossier carefully before accepting the assignment. He knew Kern as well as anyone could, but that knowledge did not include understanding. How a man could delight in violence and motiveless treachery was beyond understanding. Yet Kern did. Irrefutable evidence lay recorded in his dossier; inference with public communication networks, for no reason; several murders, all unexplainable in rational terms; fantastic public escapades, such as his somehow forcing the Melanian governor's wife to disrobe at the height of the Spring Renewal Rites, just as the priests had begun the most solemn of absolutions. Though Kern's powers were as yet undefined, his insanity was clear.

For reasons the medicos were still trying to explain, mental instability and abnormal psi-powers always seemed partners. Paranoids are perceptives in a limited way, gleaning from the thoughts of those around them only the violence and hatred that remain subliminal in healthy minds. Poltergeist phenomenon occurs only in the presence of the psi-gifted and aberrant who recognize neither of those traits in themselves. But the proportions of psi-power and instability vary with the individual. Most of the precogs or telepaths on Melan— a minute proportion of the populace—were merely eccentric. Because they devoted their skills to socially beneficial ends, people ignored their eccentricities. And when extreme psi-gifts combined with the self-awareness of social deviation, the most fully gifted usually drove themselves into a kind of self-induced catatonia. They were thus no problem.

Yet there was Kern. Undoubtedly the strongest gift ever recorded in Melanian medical history, his powers had led to insanity but not to self-censure. It the word "anti-social" had any absolute meaning, it meant "Kern." Radnor had formulated a theory about it after reading the dossier, but the medicos had refused to listen. Kern was still a child, no matter his physiological age. That had to be it. In some corner of the quagmire that might be called Kern's mind lurked a malevolent child, a demonic imp who delighted in grotesque pranks and lacked any touch of the most rudimentary conscience.

But Radnor's theory had not prepared him for meeting his prisoner. He had found Kern cradled in a body-rack behind the silver-wired grid of a psi-shield, where the medicos had strapped him after capturing him in his sleep. Radnor's gorge rose at the memory; a huge lizard exuding its fetid saurian stench, its abdomen ripped open to display the swarming, bloody mass of twisted intestines, had greeted him with a wordless keening cry. For a moment. The raucous laugh that was really Kern had echoed through the ship and the lizard had faded from sight to reveal Kern sitting there behind his pleased smirk. Just as he sat now.

He was handsome, Radnor admitted, though he disliked finding anything about the prisoner he could admire—close cropped blond curls, brilliant, almost electric, blue eyes; Kern looked like a tri-di of the All-Man, which Radnor had seen so many times floating above the altar in every Melanian temple.

Handsome was not an adequate word. Commanding, charismatic, dynamic—all of these came nearer the mood Radnor felt laving over him as he stared at the prisoner.

But even as he stared, he knew that Kern might look nothing at all as he now appeared. That was the distinctive mark of the man's powers. As far as the medicos had been able to establish, Kern wasn't precog, showed no evidence of telepathic or telekinetic powers, lacked most of the usual abilities one expected to find. He was instead a chameleon, able to change appearance at will. No one knew whether he literally changed form or only seemed to. Even in sleep his features shifted slightly. What inconclusive physiological examination the medicos had been able to perform proved nothing. If anyone touched him he shimmered through a whole range of shapes, occasionally human, more often animal. A psi-shield damped that ability but could not cancel it out, proof in itself of the man's powers.

Radnor was not even certain of Kern's gender. He had seen him once as a provocative nude girl, motioning toward him and pleading with wordless keening sounds. But that had been moments after takeoff. Then Radnor had been fresh, wary, not as strangely tired as he now felt. The deceit had failed—intellect overcoming what his glands had urged—

and had even served as a memorable warning. With the long journey from Melan to the psi-test center still ahead, he had tried to avoid looking at Kern, except when feeding him. They had a month together in the tiny ship and Radnor was determined to see his cargo safely in the hands of the psi-specialists. Let them figure Kern out.

Still, the current resemblance between Kern and the All-Man was uncanny, even if it were merely a momentary shape Kern had assumed. The fact that the likeness was so striking argued a logical mind underlying the transformation. The dossier spoke of Kern's totally random behavior. Radnor no longer accepted that evaluation; Kern obviously chose his disguises carefully, could calculate intended effect and was therefore even more dangerous than the medicos knew. Radnor stared at the bronzed, muscular form straining at the bonds behind the shield. How could such foulness appear so outwardly benign?

He snorted at his own maudlin feelings and recognized unbidden sympathy coursing through him. He knew better than to become involved with a prisoner; all bailiffs knew better. His job was merely to capture if necessary, to transport, but not to judge. Let the medicos examine and cure Kern. It was none of his business, no matter how curious he might be. But how, for example, could Kern sit immobile for hours at a time?

Radnor stared. A slight haze swept over Kern's features, defocusing him momentarily. Could he be in the act of shifting to some new form? Radnor peered more closely, unable to look away, fascinated by what the next few moments might show him. A faint noise at his back irritated him; something was interfering with his concentration. He swept an angry hand over is face and drew it away in shock. He was drenched—perspiration was pouring down his forehead.

He glanced away from Kern to the soaked palm of his own hand and as he did he saw—out of the corner of his now distracted eye—that the prisoner's body rack was empty! He quickly looked back to see Kern in place, still immobile, but shimmering and insubstantial. *A trick* . . . the thought hit him.

A faint shadow waving. A sound behind him. Then Kern struck.

Radnor fell heavily to the deck at the explosion inside his skull. Calling on every scintilla of concentration, he hung grimly onto consciousness and lurched upright to one knee. He turned toward the pain in time to glimpse a huddled figure hurling itself into the escape capsule. Then the airlock iris cycled and Kern was gone.

Radnor gave in to unconsciousness.

He woke to find himself kneeling beside the control console, one hand already on the scanner switch. He fought to ignore the pounding inside his head. He crawled onto the command cot and simultaneously activated the scanners. Through luck—or some instinct Radnor couldn't name—Kern had chosen the right instant to effect his escape. The capsule plummeted to Sol Three, the only habitable planet in that system and the nearest possible hiding place. So the man did have a touch of the telepath in him, after all; he was clearly acting on Radnor's knowledge.

Radnor thought of his Division Chief's reaction. There went the Bailiff Corps' proud reputation, flitting away because of his inattention—no escapes in over two centuries—and now this. Worse, Kern was making straight for an interdicted system and its primitive world. There was no telling what a disruptive force he might prove. And to demonstrate space flight to primitives! The potential culture shock was inconceivable. All societies lacking nuclear power and interplanetary travel—Sol Three among them—were under automatic interdiction.

Radnor hesitated only a moment. For atmosphere entry alone, he might well be busted from the Corps, his career as Bailiff ruined. But if Kern escaped...

He refused to consider it. He locked his tracer beam on the capsule growing smaller every second in the ship's scanners and offered up a small prayer of apology as his ship dove lower, dragging down Radnor's future with it.

Kern headed for the nightside, arching toward the northern hemisphere. Radnor closed the gap. The escape capsule lacked the speed to lose its pursuer, but its lead now looked insurmountable. Radnor pushed his ship to the limits of safe entry velocity—not enough. He switched from praying to cursing—perhaps less effective but certainly more satisfying—and reached beneath the command cot for his huntpack, which he checked quickly as the ship blazed its way into the heavy atmosphere. Tranquilizer darts; stunner, fully charged; shiplink beacon; pitons and elastisteel line; the pouch of diamonds, acceptable exchange anywhere in the known universe, though Radnor planned never to be in the position of having to contact a native for anything so risky as face-to-face trading; infrared beam and goggles; concentrated food for several days; psi-detector; and the forcefield pack casing itself—everything in place and operational.

He flipped the bow scanner to full magnification and watched the capsule heading for the lower tip of a huge lake which glimmered flat in the light of Sol Three's single moon.

Then he saw the rockets flare as the capsule blasted against gravity's pull and settled to a thundering crash near the lake. The capsule, unlike Radnor's ship, lacked anti-grav and depended for landing upon simple thrust engines, a fact that now gave Radnor a target, a spot glowing orange-blue in the night. He slowed to land near the flames licking around the capsule's touchdown point, only to freeze in momentary horror. A scant five thousand meters above the surface, he saw below him row upon row of faint lights winking in the darkness. Kern had landed in the midst of a settlement.

Radnor reacted quickly, allowing the automatics to seek out a clear area and waft his ship gently to the surface. Full refrigeration cooled the ship's hull as it descended and Radnor waited for anchored stability before cycling the exterior hatch.

He peered cautiously at his surroundings. Through the goggles now fitted close over his eyes, he watched the pool of infrared from his helmet beam illuminate the ground around him. His ship sat beside a squat building some eight meters high, only slightly shorter than the ship itself. On all sides similar buildings reared their crude shapes in the darkness, all apparently of unpainted, wooden construction, all approximately square. They presented little problem. He spun the rheostat which controlled the ship's surface spectrum until a shrill whine sounded in his ears. He locked the rheostat. His ship now matched the surrounding buildings in color and apparent texture. In the dark—he fervently hoped—no one would notice. And he could be gone by morning.

He gritted his teeth. He *would* be gone by morning!

His last airborne glimpse of the capsule's impact area had told him that less than a kilometer separated him from his quarry. He moved in that direction, huddling close to the wooden buildings as he did. A brief check of his shiplink beacon reassured him. It homed on the disguised ship and would serve to lead him back, if he became disoriented in these unfamiliar surroundings.

He located a street which led toward the flames now lighting the night sky at the point of Kern's touchdown. He stepped forward, then ducked back as two men passed in animated conversation. He understood nothing of what they said—nor did he plan to spend the hours necessary to learn their language through the ship's translator banks—but their agitation was clear. They pointed toward the fire and broke into a quick trot.

Others joined them, boiling out of the small buildings which lined the dirt street, buildings all square, all squat, all nondescript. At least one problem had solved itself: the people's garments were not particularly unusual, most of them two-piece arrangements of shirt and trousers. The women wore long skirts which swept the dusty board sidewalks. Radnor decided his neutral gray coverall would pass, at least in the dark. And happily not all the men he saw were bearded.

He stowed the goggles and infrared beam back in his pack; gas lanterns potted at intervals along the winding street provided sufficient light.

Keeping apart from the crowd which milled down the length of the street, he followed. Then a strange clamor drove him into a doorway where he waited. A steaming boiler drawn by four large quadrupeds rattled past. The clanging noise sounded from a large bell mounted atop the boiler, shaken by one of the men who clung recklessly to the side of the careening cart. It looked to be some sort of steam pump, though

Radnor wasn't certain. But now he knew why this world was laid under interdict. Apparently it lacked even internal combustion engines, let alone atomic power. He thought once more of his pending promotion and sighed. If he got out of this mess without being discovered...

He covered nearly a kilometer before reaching the fire. It had already spread to several buildings along the riverfront but seemed to be under control. Fire fighters concentrated in containing the flames, spraying water on the surrounding buildings.

He couldn't approach the center of the blaze, not with the crowd gathered between him and the light, so he contented himself with trying to understand the crowd's behavior. Every few moments a man or boy would burst through the wall of people standing before him and dash past, carrying bulky fabric sacks looted from the fire area. When one of the sacks split and spilled on the street, Radnor snatched up a piece of its contents: compressed carbon, a primitive fuel. And that accounted for the heat of the blaze now illuminating the sky overhead. Kern had landed in or near a fuel storage area. Huge piles of the carbon burned with great intensity, sending up acrid fumes and flickering blue lights. With any luck the capsule might already be consumed in the blaze. And that would solve another problem.

For an instant Radnor almost gave in to the wild hope that Kern, too, might have been trapped in the pyre, but he could not bring himself to wish the extinction of any sentient creature, even one so patently mad as Kern.

He drew the psi-detector from his pack and stared at the directional indicator. If Kern lived, he was out of range. Luckily no one else in the crowd registered the slightest quiver on the detector's gauge. That would have been the end of his hunt, Radnor knew, to discover that these primitives possessed measurable psi-powers. He almost smiled; things were looking up.

He began the hunt.

Keeping as near the blaze as caution would allow, he circled to the north, to his left. The fire had been contained, confined to four blocks of fuel depot and wharves. The river to the east had saved the fire fighters a good share of their work; it also cut the arc of Radnor's search to a mere hundred and eighty degrees.

He circled left to the water's edge, then doubled back to retrace his steps and scout the south half of the semicircle mapped out in his mind. The streets here were cobblestoned, the buildings larger but still of wooden construction. Passersby ignored him, more involved in shouting greetings to one another and waving bottles—apparently some intoxicant. He sensed festival in the crowd's mood.

The southern arc of his search failed to draw any indication on the psi-detector. Several times he stepped into doorways to avoid knots of men who roamed the streets, singing and shouting. And then he saw a flicker on his gauge; it pointed back the way he had come, back toward the ship. As he turned to move in that direction a trio of men accosted him boisterously, but he avoided their grasp and ducked around a corner—and into the arms of a fleshy, flaccid woman with straw-colored hair and red dye smeared across her mouth. He recoiled from her touch before recognizing her for what she was. The night women on Melan shaved their heads—he tried not to judge; cultures differ. He pushed past her just as she changed appearance before his eyes, the straw-colored hair giving way to a shaven, gilded skull.

He snatched out the stunner, but Kern was gone into the darkness. Radnor cursed again and followed.

It's a game to him. He is playing tag with me . . .

Radnor swung into an easy lope, glancing at the psi-detector's wobbling needle every few yards. Once he stumbled over a loose board in the sidewalk and heard Kern's raucous laughter from the darkness ahead. Kern was leading him back toward his own ship.

It was hard to tell who dictated the game, he or Kern. And it was becoming obvious he was in real trouble—how would he recapture someone he couldn't even recognize? Behind him pale light streaked the horizon above the ramshackle shanties. Morning soon. And what then? He mentally tested a few feeble excuses, trying to invent one his Division Chief might accept. None existed. It was find Kern, or else.

He recognized buildings as he ran; he had come this way toward the fire. But how could Kern know where the ship lay hidden? He couldn't see through the camouflage. Perhaps his powers included area-sensing. He had been aboard the ship long enough to familiarize himself with the aura of its electronic equipment, even though the dossier hadn't so much as hinted at such talents.

Nova the dossier! And nova the medicos. . . .

No one but Radnor knew a thing about Kern. And Radnor knew nothing certain any longer—nothing more than Kern's teasing him, a spoiled child playing a game.

He sprinted along the dimly lighted street, scrambling awkwardly through a pile of discarded bottles and trash which lay in his path as he cut across an empty lot toward the ship. No one was there ahead of him.

He paused to check the detector again. Motionless. But how? He knew Kern was nearby, sensed it. *Stop*, he told himself. *Think it out. Why did* ...

A door burst open to his left and sent him diving to the ground, stunner in his hand. A quarrel poured through the open door and followed a heavy-set woman into the pre-dawn paleness. She carried a metal container and shouted something over her shoulder as she walked toward the squat building beside which Radnor's ship stood. He waited quietly when she paused to glance at his disguised ship in bewilderment, then turned to shake her fist at the deep voice which pursued her from the house.

She walked on and Radnor relaxed. He watched her enter the shabby structure, then lay thinking.

I know Kern's not dead. Can he be asleep?

Radnor glared at the sunlight slowly spreading it way up the side of his ship, then shook his head in resignation. He didn't dare a liftoff in full daylight; someone would certainly see. And that meant he would have to wait till dark, either that or destroy the ship and sentence himself to live out his life in this barbaric settlement. Worse, such an action would consign Kern to their midst as well.

When matters reached the stage of full dilemma, Radnor knew what to do. Nothing. He stopped planning.

Let things happen, then react....

The deep voice roared through the lighted doorway once more and Radnor treated himself to the luxury of shouting a tired curse in answer before entering is ship.

Darkness settled. Radnor had spent the day in edgy rest, waiting for Kern's next move. All alarm systems were rigged but no one had approached the ship closer than a few meters. Radnor had not wasted his irritating leisure. Turning the ship's audible receivers to full power, he had lain in half-sleep while the ship's translator banks accumulated, parsed, analyzed and taught him the language. "English," the primitives called it, a complex system but not impossible to grasp. Radnor grinned wryly; he could return to Melan, the Bailiff Corps only expert in this "English," a skill calculated to get him sacked rather than admired.

Overheard conversations had provided him with interesting food for speculation. The night before had indeed been a sort of festival which recurred each seventh day. Called "Satyr-day" in English, it signaled free rein to licentiousness for a brief time, followed in turn by "Sun-day," the day of recovery from Satyr-day's excesses. People whose voices came through the ship's receivers boasted of clan warfare between locals and members of some civic subdivisions called "Conley's Patch" (named apparently for a resident) and "Kilgubbin" (untranslatable) to the northeast.

But none of the information helped Radnor locate Kern, who remained hidden somewhere nearby. At dusk the buxom woman of the early morning had once more briefly interrupted her continuing quarrel with her mate to visit their "barn" (a building for storing grain and foodstuffs, housing livestock). Other than that, the day had passed quietly. No one took special notice of his ship, a fact that he laid to the primitives' state of misery hanging on from the revels of Satyr-day.

When darkness completed itself, Radnor finished his preparations and left the ship, leaving behind his huntpack. Even its forcefield was unnecessary; Kern had no physical weapons, no weapons at all, in fact except himself. And Radnor now knew more about that "self." It was the very weapon he would use against Kern.

Having watched people enter and leave several of the shanties in the neighborhood, he grew certain that Kern hid in the "barn." It had remained deserted all day, except for the owner's brief visit, and Kern would certainly have chosen the best possible hiding place for the game he now played. He was waiting to oust Radnor from the ship and take command himself—"Hill Governor," they had called the game in Radnor's youth.

He stalked Kern slowly, trusting now to the indefinable tingle he had come to associate with Kern's presence aboard the ship. He moved toward the barn in a slow, arcing path, keeping between the barn exit and the ship.

Must keep Kern from the ship. Suppress all other thoughts. Keep Kern from the ship or he'll escape . . .

The barn door slid open easily at his touch and he peered into the musky darkness. The feeling was stronger. Kern was . . .

Keep Kern from the ship or he'll take off without me. It's easy to fly it. Anyone can fly it. Keep Kern from the ship . . . .

He stepped inside. Shadows flickered along the far wall, cast in the light of a petroleum lantern left hanging on a hook inside the door. Kern was nowhere in sight. Several feathered bipeds ("chickens") clucked and scratched at the dusty floor.

Don't let Kern get to the ship. The red switch activates antigrav. If Kern lies on the command cot and hits that switch . . . Keep Kern from the ship . . .

Two cows (mature female bovine, genus *Bos*) swung their sad eyes toward him and lowed quietly. Radnor moved toward the far end of the barn, peering carefully into the dark corners.

Where would he hide? What form has he—DON'T! Don't suspect. Keep Kern from the ship. Easy to fly. Freedom that way. Win the game. Finders keepers...

He inched slowly through the swirling dust, carefully turning his back to the door and forcing himself not to think. *To think, to think, to think...*

It happened. Kern's wild laugh echoed behind him, but Radnor willed himself still, not moving, giving Kern the chance to run. He turned then and saw one of the cows rise up on her/its/his hind legs and shift form, now Kern, now not-Kern. And Kern made his break. Radnor walked slowly toward her/it/him, thinking, *Safe it he gets to the ship. Nothing to stop him. The ship and escape...*

But he had misjudged his quarry. Not content merely to flee, Kern snatched the lantern from its hook with one hand/hoof—and hurled it. Radnor ducked as the petroleum spewed across the wooden floor and scattered a carpet of golden flames washing through the tinder-dry refuse toward him. A curtain of fire rose instantly to the rafters and cut off Radnor's escape. But he whirled and kicked out a wooden shutter, then dove through the opening as Kern rounded the corner of the barn, sprinting now on two legs, shifting appearance in the ghostly light that flickered through the cracks in the barn wall.

Radnor heard, *I win!* echo in his mind's ear. He hit the hatch opening an instant before it cycled shut. He was inside, thinking, *Kern's free. He'll escape. The red switch. Lie on the cot and hit the red switch...*

He flinched in the deluge of laughter pouring over him and watched Kern, now the bronzed All-Man again, dive to the couch and slam a palm against the anti-grav activator. And against the tranquilizer dart imbedded there, point up. Kern lunged back in anger, but too late. Elastisteel webbing fell from overhead and pinioned him to the command cot, where he struggled violently as the ship lifted. Then his struggles grew weaker as his body betrayed him. Only his mind reached out to Radnor, crying, *Cheating! Cheating! I won!*

Radnor ducked behind the psi-shield and protected himself with mentally recited paradigms: *I am, you are, he is, we are, you are, they are . . .*

When Kern's thrashing subsided Radnor inched out from behind the psi-shield and bound his prisoner, this time in coil after coil of elastisteel line. He propped and strapped Kern once more in the body rack and vowed not to exchange so much as a glance with him until touchdown at the psi-test asteroid. Let the medicos take over then.

A few days more and the assignment would end, a few days in which to rehearse his testimony. If he could persuade the Division Chief that he had saved the Corps' reputation against impossible odds he might not be drummed out in disgrace. And as for violating the interdiction, well—no harm done.

CODA:

THREE HUNDRED DEAD THOUSANDS
HOMELESS IN DISASTROUS FIRE
Special to The Clarion

CHICAGO, Monday, October 9, 1871—Yesterday's blaze still rages out of control in the West and South Divisions. Various authorities have blamed labor agitators, a group of the city's Irish pilfering in the dead of night or other unnamed agents. Mr. Padraic Sweeney of 2240 DeKoven St. reports having seen a cow upset a lantern which ignited the O'Leary barn. Mrs. O'Leary denies it, claiming instead that lightning struck the barn at 9:30 P.M.

Police suspect the same party or parties unknown who set Saturday night's mysterious fire between Canal and Clinton Streets. They are investigating and expect to make arrests shortly...

The Man Who Faded Away

first published in *Fantastic Science Fiction and Fantasy Stories,* June 1971

On a Friday morning Harry Ferguson decided to stay in bed. That fact, in and of itself, was not newsworthy. What makes it worth recording is that Harry Ferguson did precisely that—stayed in bed. Every day for the past three months he had wanted to remain in bed. But never once had he done so. Today was the day. No phone call to the office. No excuses. No mock-cold or fraudulent headache. Harry simply wanted to stay at home. He had realized only the night before that he was fading away.

Walking up the fourteen steps to the brownstone where his furnished room awaited him, Harry had spoken to Mrs. Briggs, his landlady. "Good evening, Mrs. Briggs," he said. She ignored him, uttered not a syllable, unless her constant asthmatic wheezing could be regarded an utterance. Nothing strange about her silence. Mrs. Briggs never spoke to Harry. But on this occasion she extended before her at arm's length a dustmop. She shook it in Harry's face.

He sneezed twice and waved a hand before him to clear away the clumps of gray cotton which hovered there. "Why did you . . . ?" But Mrs. Briggs had walked back inside. At that instant Harry Ferguson recognized a fact he had long tried to ignore. No one ever saw Harry Ferguson.

Not only was he easy to ignore, he had been that for all his 42 years. But lately, no one had seen him to ignore him. They gazed straight through Harry Ferguson as if he were an insubstantial wraith.

At the office, for instance, there was his supervisor, Mr. Schaeffer. Mr. Schaeffer walked past Harry's desk several times each day. He never said hello. He never even nodded. Harry arrived precisely at 8:58 AM, sat down, opened an envelope that lay on his desk. The envelope was always there. Someone left it before 8:58 AM. Harry removed from the envelope the lists of figures awaiting his attention, spent the day recording the figures in a ledger which he then replaced in the envelope. After Harry left the office at 5:02 PM, someone collected the ledger, in its envelope, and sent it elsewhere. During each of the days he spent in this fashion, no one said a word to Harry Ferguson.

On Friday morning, Harry remained in bed until 10:30 A.M. He did not sleep.

The he arose and made a pot of coffee. He decided to review the evidence. There was no real starting point. In school, teachers had sent notes telling his mother of Harry's cooperation—assignments in on time, never a bit of trouble in department. Harry was a model student.

He was also the butt of several unpleasant jokes, two of which he could remember. The Barton girl had once said, "Harry? He blends with the wallpaper." And her friends, May Schwartz, had answered, "Ain't that the truth for God's sake! When Harry comes into the room, you think somebody left." Their laughter was not malicious. They had no intention of hurting Harry Ferguson. They simply did not see him standing beside them.

Harry grew more aware of his problem when he began to date. Her name was Carolyn Stern. Even after their third date, when he ran into her in the park one day and walked over to say hello, she looked blankly at him and said, "Yes?" It made him feel like the Avon lady.

"Harry Ferguson. Remember? We went skating last month."

"Harry? Oh sure, Harry. How are you?" and she wandered off without waiting for an answer. He didn't really mind. He favored the quiet life.

For the first few months at Acme Actuarials he had jotted down the random names by which Mr. Schaeffer addressed him. Ferris, twice. Then there was Feeny, and Folsom, Jorgenson and Torgenson. Once Finstermacher. Even Halpern, though Harry could not account for that one. But for the past few months Mr. Schaeffer hadn't said a word. Harry knew in his heart the man meant nothing by it. He simply didn't see Harry sitting there.

Walking to the mirror with his cup of coffee, Harry examined himself. It was not true that he was colorless. He could see that much. He may have looked average, but not everyone had a wave in his thinning, sandy-colored hair. One of Harry's teeth hung crooked—he opened his mouth wider and stared—but probably too far back to be noticed. His eyes were grey, but look there—several freckles. What's-his-name had freckles—Ron Howard, the movie kid—and people remembered him. Harry had once tried to grow a moustache. After no one remarked on it for several weeks he grew tired of trimming it and shaved it off. But no one noticed that either. The pale strip soon faded, or darkened, or whatever the right word was. Then there remained no trace of Harry Ferguson's attempt to escape anonymity.

Harry looked at his watch. Nearly 11:30 AM. By now he should have completed nearly half his daily quota of lists. Perhaps someone would notice when he came around after five to collect the envelope of completed punch cards. And noticing Harry's absence would be almost like noticing his presence, wouldn't it? Harry thought so.

Because he had an hour before he could carry out his plan, he made a peanut butter and jelly sandwich and turned on the TV. It was a quiz game. Harry knew most of the answers, no one had ever called him stupid. Maybe that was another part of his problem. If he were stupid, they might get angry with him. But he wasn't. And they didn't.

He once blamed his parents for the way he was. As if he didn't have enough burdens, then to find himself the only man he knew without a middle name. He had heard a joke in the army. He'd spent two years as a private, permanently awaiting orders. The joke was about a man who had no name, only initials. L.B. Those were the initials. But when they gave him dogtags, they wrote it "Johnson, L(only) B(only)." After that everyone called him Lonely Bonely. Harry had no middle name. His dogtags read "Ferguson, Harry (nmn), for "no middle name." There was no way to make a joke out of (nmn).

A woman on TV pointed a finger at him and asked, "Do you have bad breath?" Harry didn't answer. It was obvious she wasn't talking to him. He turned off the TV.

Last night, after Mrs. Briggs had not seen him and the fact of his problem had become something he could no longer ignore, Harry went out to test his theory. The idea was ridiculous. No one is invisible, he told himself. To prove it, he walked two blocks to Shimer's Department Store. On the third floor he found the lingerie counter. No other men anywhere in sight. He waited a full twenty minutes for a saleslady to notice him and ask what he wanted. None did.

Harry made one final attempt. He walked into a dressing room at the end of the floor. A saleslady stood with her arms folded while a remarkably-built young woman tried on a kind of bra that stretched from waist toward her shoulders but had no straps. When she took it off portions of her chest slipped and she was no longer remarkably-built. Harry politely removed his hat. First the saleslady looked toward Harry and looked away. The young woman looked at him but quickly glanced at the saleslady and then shook her head. She grew pale and several times glanced in Harry's direction. But he knew from the way she behaved that—after the first glance—she couldn't see him. She tried on another of the long bras. Harry debated speaking to them, but he saw no reason to embarrass anyone. Instead, he walked out and went home.

In the street two cars almost ran him down. One was a cab. The driver failed to scream curses out his open window at Harry. That clinched it. He had faded away.

Now there remained only the project he had devised. He could not prove he was visible. Perhaps he could prove he was not visible.

Harry arrived at the Mercantile Savings Bank too early. Therefore he walked once more around the block. In his pocket he carried the cap pistol Mrs. Briggs' son had left on the stairs. Harry had found it. He meant to return it, he no longer had a use for it.

When the clock outside the bank showed 12:58 PM Harry went inside. One o'clock should be the busiest time of the day, he had reasoned. Friday. Employers picking up payrolls. Employees cashing payroll checks or drawing out funds for the weekend. Yes, he told himself, the busiest time of the day.

He walked directly to the center one of nine barred windows. He pushed his pistol between the bars toward the girl who stood chewing her gum with unconcerned violence.

"This is a stick-up," he said. He had heard it put that way on the TV. "Give me all your money. Big bills." He hesitated for a moment because the next word troubled him. But Harry was a methodical man. "Sister." On the TV they always called girls, "sister."

Her eyes grew round and her mouth hung slack. Harry looked away. He could see the lump of pink gum lying on her tongue, and he didn't want to embarrass her. The girl stared at Harry's cap pistol. Really, Johnny Brigg's cap pistol. Harry was only using it at the moment. She took the brown paper bag he pushed across to her and filled it with bundles of money fastened together with those grayish-blue strips of paper.

Harry said, "Thank you," and started to walk away. He stepped back. "Sister," he said. The he continued on to the door.

He was nearly half-way there when he heard her start to scream in a surprisingly clear and effective way. Surprising, considering the large lump of gum in her mouth. Almost immediately a loud siren assaulted his ears. Harry began to wonder whether proving his point was really worth all the commotion it was causing around him. Half the people ran toward the street, half toward the girl who was screaming. Many of the runners jostled Harry and pushed him to one side. He walked calmly through the confusion and out onto the street where he stopped to watch.

In moments a police car squealed to a stop before the bank. Two officers ran in with drawn guns. Seeing them made Harry remember something. He still held Johnny Briggs' cap pistol in his right hand. He put it inside the bag with the money. He took time to admire the speed with which the police had arrived. Then he walked home.

Saturday's papers spoke of the daring holdup. "Broad daylight" was the phrase they used. Harry laid down the paper for a moment to wonder at that phrase. He could find nothing in his experience to account for the association of "broad" and "daylight." He couldn't imagine "narrow daylight." It didn't really matter. He only wondered at the lack of precision in diction.

He shrugged and read the rest of the story. The girl described Johnny Briggs' cap pistol in vivid detail. She could not describe Harry, except to say that he looked average. He nodded with some satisfaction—she had seen him, or now thought she had. Then near the end of the column he found what he was looking for. The girl had triggered the bank's automatic cameras with her foot. When developed, the film showed only a smear where Harry had stood. It was overexposed or under-exposed. Different accounts disagreed on that point. For Harry's purposes, it didn't really matter. He knew they wouldn't see him.

Monday morning at 10:30 he walked into the precinct station house and surrendered. He handed them the paper bag. It contained nine thousand four hundred and twelve dollars, *not*—Harry was careful to point out—"more than ten thousand," as the newspapers had claimed. If there was one thing Harry Ferguson knew, it was figures.

He confessed everything. They put him in a cell with a drunk.

Tuesday morning they came to his cell and took the drunk away. Harry shouted several times before the policeman returned the drunk and took him instead.

Inside the courtroom, Harry only shook his head when a photographer tried to take his picture. But he refused to argue with the man. Who would believe it?

They brought in the girl from the bank. Harry recognized her at once. "That's her," he said. "That's the woman I saw."

He told the judge he wanted to plead guilty. The judge asked him to wait, because this was only a preliminary hearing. The girl was asked to point him out. She couldn't. After an Assistant District Attorney whispered in her ear, she looked puzzled a moment. He whispered to her again. This time she nodded and pointed at the bench where Harry sat between two plain-clothes detectives. The judge asked him to stand. Harry did.

The girls said, "No. The tall one."

Several people in the courtroom snickered. The plain-clothes detective on Harry's right stood up. Harry could tell from the redness around the man's collar that he didn't like it. The Assistant District Attorney whispered to the girl again, while the detective stood there and everyone laughed at him.

Harry left. It was not working as he had hoped. He had already missed two full days of work and part of another. It would not do to make Mr. Schaeffer angry with him, if Mr. Schaeffer happened to notice. No one bothered Harry as he walked from the courtroom.

At his desk on the ninth floor of Acme Actuarials, he found three envelopes waiting for him. One from Friday, one from Monday, one from today. Mr. Schaeffer was walking past as Harry sat down to his desk. Harry knew he could not finish three days' work in one afternoon, not if he wanted to do his usual accurate job. He waved at Mr. Schaeffer.

"Mr. Schaeffer?" he called out.

Mr. Schaeffer stopped and looked around with a most puzzled expression on his face.

"Here!" Harry waved his hand again.

Mr. Schaffer cocked his head toward Harry. It was difficult to tell whether he saw Harry or only looked in his direction. Harry took the chance. "Mr. Schaeffer? I can't finish all this work today."

Mr. Schaeffer waved his hand. "Good work, Feldman." He walked on into his office.

I tried to tell him, Harry assured himself.

That evening the late editions told of the bank robber's daring escape from Magistrate's Court in "broad daylight." Police were confident they would soon have the man back in custody. They asked all public-spirited citizens to phone in any information on the whereabouts of a man named Harvey Finegold.

Harry Ferguson shook his head. The next time he would spend some of the money before he took the rest back. Perhaps then they'd pay attention. Yes, he would certainly do that.

commuter special

first published in *Amazing Science Fiction Stories*, January 1972

Max Ten-Smith shuffled awkwardly from the subwalk's speeding mid-strip to the slow-strip as he neared his train platform. He accidentally jostled a young woman who glared at him but maintained proper silence. Rounding the curve, they both skipped to the loading platform at the same instant, and he trod on her instep.

"Sorry," he muttered.

"You ought to be. A new pair of shoes and . . ."

QUIET PLEASE. NO TALKING.

The Voice crackled in their ears, and several heads swung their way in anger as all the other commuters entering the station flinched at the sound lancing through their concentration.

The young woman ducked instinctively and clapped a hand to her public ear. "Ohhhh!"

Max leaned closer and whispered, "It gets louder as you get older," then grinned at the hate-filled glare she threw him.

He dropped back three places in line and fell in behind another man before shuffling forward once more toward the loading ramps. One of the omnipresent car-touts waved a printed list in his face, but Max shoved him away angrily. He tried to avoid ever seeing one of the tout's time-tables. Ghouls like that disgusted him, making their living by collecting and publishing the lists of worker-eliminations.

It wasn't even legal, though The Voice overlooked it. Since commuters were determined to buy the lists, legal or not, The Voice tacitly sanctioned the slimy peddlers who stayed off the dole by selling them. So long as official doctrine still preached free enterprise, to force the car-touts out of business would hardly square with announced policy.

The queue shuffled forward another fifteen feet as the 6:05 pulled from the station. Max could recall his grandfather's complaints about trains that never ran on time. At least that problem had been solved. Every five minutes one of the stainless steel tubes hissed from the Washington station. Delay was unthinkable. Even a slight lag in departure time would throw off each subsequent train until lost seconds accumulated into minutes. And lost minutes meant collision—the certain deaths of all two thousand commuters in the pair of driverless trains which hurtled through the underground darkness at 180 mph. But such an accident was inconceivable; The Voice would see to that. Two hundred deaths remained the legal simultaneous maximum (although Max had heard a report of two cars on the same train chosen for elimination—*probably a lie*, he assured himself).

KEEP THE LINE MOVING, PLEASE.

Max glanced around. He had maintained the proper two-foot interval on the man ahead in line. Somewhere behind him a dawdler had drawn the rebuke, heard by all of them of course. A Senator had recently introduced a bill to make the newest ear inserts selective, different frequencies for different occupations, or age groups—Max wasn't clear on that point. He'd know more after the bill passed and The Voice allowed it merits to be explained to the people.

He certainly hoped it passed. His son Bobby would be registering for tele-school soon, and on that same day The Voice surgical staff would place the ear-insert in Bobby's public ear and issue him his work number. It wasn't too bad for a child. Max repeated this for the hundredth time. Not as painful as it had been when he'd undergone surgery (and used both days of his annual sick-leave to recover).

For the hundredth time he wondered whether the inescapable rumors were true—that workers above Five-level had removable inserts and could enjoy occasional aural privacy. Possibly. If he ever met a Five-level, that's the first thing he'd ask.

The 6:10 hissed to a stop at the platform and its doors split open with a pneumatic gasp. The line moved forward uncertainly for a few feet as it divided into five short lines leading to the open doors. Suddenly a man near the front broke free and ran shouting back toward the subwalk.

Instinctively Max dropped to his knees with the others before the high frequency whine pierced his eardrum. The running man stumbled and fell at the pain they all felt, and from nowhere two guards moved to jerk him erect and drag him once more to his place in line.

No one met his pleading gaze.

Certainly, we're all afraid, Max admitted silently. *But not like that. Thank God we're more civilized than that.*

No commuter enjoyed this part of his daily routine. Yet few let their fear master them. They muttered the cliché about gas and taxes, then shuffled into the tube cars. The odds against choosing one of the eliminator cars were comforting. With a train every five minutes, five cars to a train, all in all a good gamble. "Remember the odds," read signs posted every few feet overhead. Many thousands to one, the newspapers all said.

Another car-tout tugged at Max's sleeve, but he shook him off brusquely. The man ahead in line bought one of the black-bordered pages and began to read it avidly. Max peered over his shoulder and scanned the lists, searching for the Washington-Philadelphia schedule. There is was: Monday, first car on the 5:15, the third at 5:25 and the fifth at 7:20. Tuesday, third car at 6:10, second at 6:55, second at 7:00, fourth at 7:15. Wednesday, fourth at 5:25. *Why was that? Why only one car eliminated Wednesday? Today's Friday. Does that mean . . ?*

But Max shook off his mood and tried to concentrate on the soothing music which had begun to melt in his ear. *Good. Fifty feet from the front of the line.* That's where the music always began, an attempt—someone had told him—to calm the more susceptible types who might panic at seeing how soon it would be their turn to enter the train.

Another thing—the touts never came this near the tracks. Max distrusted their predictions anyway. Some of them used astrology, others searched for mathematical patterns in the lists of recent eliminations. Yet everyone knew that The Voice selected cards entirely at random. It was foolish to try to predict which compartment was marked on any given train. The only certainty lay in the averages—in the ten years since elimination had been made law, since 1 Nov. 2033, The Voice had selected an average of three cars a night on the Washington-Philadelphia line. Three cars, two hundred workers each—six hundred people. Nowhere near as bad as the New York-Philadelphia run. There the average surpassed four cars a night. And still the population rose.

That fact wasn't common knowledge, but Max knew. He knew too well. He was several days behind in processing orders for food-servo equipment in the new apartment complex being constructed in the Allentown section of central Philadelphia. But he had heard nothing to suggest that The Voice would extend eliminations to other commuter lines (if only there were some occupation-office located in Pittsburgh that might hire someone like him, a man was a bare Ph.D. and only nine technical pamphlets published. Not a real book to his name.)

For a moment, Max wondered why The Voice never chose a morning train. *Probably disturb people,* he thought, *seeing the darkened cars on their way to the office. Nobody'd put in a good day's work that way.* Whatever the reasons, he was happy he had wangled the transfer from New York to Washington after his promotion to Ten-Smith. He knew he had no chance to make Five-level, not with only a year to go till retirement. That eminence was for younger men, not someone nearing forty.

PLEASE KEEP MOVING.

The Voice sounded jovial, more cheerful as Max neared the loading platform. Was that a sign? Or was it intended to deceive? Again he cut short his thoughts and tried to recall the details of a story he had heard only that morning. He had to decide whether or not to tell Mary when he got home.

Probably not true, but worth investigating. A man in meat distribution claimed to have discovered a way of commuting from Philadelphia to Washington entirely by local trains. It took him five hours each way, but even with a full six-hour day sandwiched in, he had plenty of time at home. And local cars were exempt from elimination, at least until The Voice could have them equipped with gas nozzles. But that would take years. Till then, the equipment on the local lines was reasonably safe.

Certainly no one would ride the locals if elimination began there as well. After the cine houses installed laughing gas equipment in a futile effort to match the seductive powers of the TV laugh track, business dropped off. Who could enjoy the cine knowing that, at any time, The Voice might take to eliminating theater crowds? Wasn't the equipment already in place? And the introduction of nozzles in local trains would signal their end too, Max was certain.

He recalled having taken locals to Chicago—a three day ride—when he put his mother in the Midwest Home. He hated the trip, but—born in the Midwest—she qualified for Senior Security nowhere else. And he certainly couldn't support her, not as a Seventeen-Smith, which he had been at the time.

The locals were terrible, stopping every few miles all the way along their route. And frighteningly empty at night, some cars carrying no more than thirty or forty people. He had slept badly, never certain when someone might ask why he hadn't taken the tube. He could have blamed it on his mother's fears, but frankly, he felt the same way. That had been before he knew the odds. And before he knew that only Fifteen-level workers and above were subject to elimination.

LOAD THE SIX-FIFTEEN, PLEASE.
THANK YOU AND GOODNIGHT.

Max shuffled forward quickly, trying to estimate whether this train would have room for him. It would be close. And if he missed this one, he might miss dinner. Forty-seven minutes on the train, nine minutes on the subwalk—add that to 6:15. It would be close. The Servo always dished out dinner at 7:15. Once Mary had tried to warm it over, but it didn't taste the same. Not that Max could complain. A man making his way up in the Servo staff was better off not knocking his own department's efficiency. The Servo would be on time; that he knew. Whether Max would be was another matter. People might be late; machines never were.

The line neared the train compartment door, and the man ahead of Max leaned back to say, "If there's room for one, you take it."

"Shhh!"

"There's nothing wrong. I just feel like waiting."

Damn hunch player, Max thought. *Or has he seen a pattern on the tout sheet? Nonsense!*

"Board, please," the guard urged them into the car.

Immediately Max recognized his error. What had he been thinking of? The wrong line! He was in the Talking Car. He hadn't made this mistake in months.

All around him the roar of voices rumbled off the car walls. Mostly the young unmarrieds who used the Talking Cars for Talk-dates, these were precisely the commuters Max detested most. Half of them would leave their straps at any excuse, walking up and down the length of the car to shout at one another. (He also admitted to jealousy—some of them looked so young to be above Fifteen-level, but they certainly must be: none of the worker classes would voluntarily ride the eliminator cars when they could sit back comfortably and wait while the ranks atop the social pyramid thinned to their benefit. But mostly, Max hated the noise.)

Even in the row of seats, limited to cripples with seat-permits, the talking was incessant. *Couldn't a man...?*

DOOR CLOSING.

Max grinned at the sudden silence as everyone in the car reacted simultaneously. He snatched the overhead strap in both hands and hung on while the tube built to topspeed. In a way it was attractive, the swaying movement as everyone clutched at his strap and tried to lean forward to minimize acceleration, then drifted upright and back in unison till they all leaned toward the rear of the car.

Counting to himself, Max estimated three minutes precisely and reversed the tension in his legs for the halt of acceleration. As slowly as they had drifted back, everyone swung upright again, and the babble started at once.

"I don't want you to think I was afraid back there or anything." A man tapped Max on the shoulder.

"What?"

"About giving you my place I mean. It wasn't that at all I just thought I'd wait for the next train."

Max nodded without meaning to agree. The man was clearly terrified; he hung onto his strap with both hands clenched knuckle-white, even though the train rode smoothly on its cushion of air and gave the impression of being stationary.

"No. I won't lie to you," the man continued. "But I heard today they're going to double up on Friday's trains. Maybe take a whole bunch of them at once."

Max turned away.

"Listen! I mean it! I'm in Census and . . ."

"Why not talk it over with someone else. I'm not interested."

"'Not interested'? Gas! Tell it to The Voice, Commuter."

"Hey! Did you hear?" a woman behind them interrupted. "They gassed a car on the 5:30. A man back there called his wife from the station, and she told him. Pass it on."

The frightened man whined. "See. What did I say? They're making Fridays a big day from now on."

Trying to calm him, Max said, "You could look at it another way. Since they eliminated one car already, that makes us even safer. Ever think of that?"

"Say! Why not?" The man brightened noticeably. "You got a point. I mean, they're not going to take another one right away, are they?"

Max debated reminding him of what they both had seen on the tout-sheet—cars eliminated on consecutive trains—but thought better of it. Before he could say another word, the man dashed toward the front of the car with the good news. And Max grabbed the ear-plug hawker who passed by. Four dollars was outrageous—he could buy them in any drugstore for less than three—but it was worth it. He inserted the plugs and drew himself inside his aural privacy.

"Privacy." Almost the forgotten commodity. In a country of four hundred fifty million people, where the east coast megalopolis stretched as one great swath of pavement from Boston to Richmond, few people could afford that luxury. That accounted for the cooperatives which hired lobbyists to keep Congress apprised of the great need. Invasion of privacy had become a crime second only to unlicensed murder in severity of punishment. Now that China and the USSR had made of each other vast radio-active deserts, there was less and less emigration room on the face of the globe. While millions starved abroad, while medical science continually extended a man's potential life-span through research, while the population swelled at such enormous speed, the lobbyists had finally accomplished their aim and solved the problem—temporarily—in the only possible way. The eliminator cars. A simple lottery of death.

Max stared at the gas nozzles which dotted the roof of the car. Most of them would never hiss out their fog. But some would. Some spewed death through cars exactly like this one every afternoon of the week. Even the weekend excursion trains had been selected in recent weeks, though less often than commuter cars. The commuter cars carried the manager class, heads of families.

And when they died, their families went to the Kansas barracks. "The heartland of America," it had once been called. No one relished the idea of families split up that way, but the alternative to the eliminator cars was mass sterilization, much less humane, everyone agreed.

Eliminating the breadwinners offered another plus: more job openings. More men able to make their way in the government, able to vote, own property, able to take part in the lottery itself. It was a reasonable system, Max reminded himself—as he did daily.

As every commuter did.

Daily.

He found himself staring, unseeing, at the gas nozzles when the car lights dimmed and interrupted his reverie. He felt rather than heard the silence which settled over the Talking Car, and he jerked loose his ear plugs. Every other commuter stood frozen, holding his breath. The lights brightened, then dimmed again. A woman screamed and that signaled permission for a great roar of protests, of mumble prayers and anguished lament. And then the lights came up to stay.

But the rest of the trip was different, as each commuter stared warily at his neighbor and at the nozzles which seemed suddenly to hang lower over their heads. Max vowed he would mention the local trains to his wife. If one man could endure the long trip each day, so could others. He would locate that man in meat distribution and ask him the way.

He might even resign. He could do that, and take Mary and Bobby to the Kansas barracks. Why not? A year till retirement, and then what? Wasn't retirement nearly the same as the dole? If he stuck out the full year, they could keep their apartment, and perhaps have enough money for an occasional trip—on the train, of course. But was it worth another year of the lottery? It would be different if they could afford their own car. Then he might see an advantage in hanging on. But the annual 100% owner's tax on automobiles put them out of reach of everyone but Senators and One-level workers.

He could at least mention it to her. He had been in the lottery nearly since the beginning, ten years of hearing The Voice, of dreading the tube. Once he had come to work to discover that Twelve-Parsons at the next desk had been eliminated. It was difficult to ignore the absence of someone he knew personally.

It simply wasn't worth it, he told himself as he stared at the nozzles.

Preoccupied, he missed seeing the sign light up and came to his sense only at The Voice.

DECELERATION IN TEN SECONDS.

He snatched quickly at the strap overhead and tensed his legs against inertia.

THIRTY SECONDS TO DISEMBARK.
PREPARE PLEASE.

The doors gasped open amid a babble of relief as people exchanged goodbyes before reaching the platform and enforced silence. Max drifted behind them, waiting for The Voice to quiet them before he risked stepping out into the mob. Yet this time the silence was self-imposed, tangible in a way that troubled him.

When he stepped from the car he saw the reason. To his left, the car ahead of his was dark. Totally, completely dark, its doors still sealed as it sat in the station. Then the guards arrived to uncouple the darkened car and shunt it off the track to whatever destination awaited selected cars.

Two hundred people? Only one car away. If I had...

"Close one, hey buddy?" the frightened commuter whispered with a grin. "What's that do to the odds?"

Max returned the smile in spite of himself. The man was right. *A near-miss like that's probably as close as I'll ever get.* He winked at his companion.

On the subwalk home through the crowded tunnel under the Philadelphia apartment complex, he felt the sudden urge to look outside, to see what the weather was like. But that could wait till he got home. He and Mary would put Bobby to bed after dinner and set the autonurse, then walk over to the window. One advantage of having Ten-rank, he merited an apartment near the outer wall of the complex. The nearest window was only five minutes away, yet they hadn't taken the walk in months.

He felt so buoyed that he chided himself for his foolish fears. *"Remember the odds,"* he recited silently. *No sense worrying Mary with that nonsense about the local trains. Probably a lie, anyway.* The shuffling slap of thousands of feet reassured him as he skipped nimbly off the subwalk and into a branching tunnel. He felt comforted to be so near home again, in familiar corridors.

Standing in line before the express elevator, he checked his watch. He would still make it in time for dinner. Seventy-five floors by express, then three in the tiny fifty-man local.

He inched forward with the others and stood precisely in the center of his painted square, nodding to a man he recognized, another Ten-level from down the corridor.

Only when the elevator lurched upward did his roving eye fasten on a strange sight. Nozzles dotted the elevator ceiling, and a whitish fog drifted down to settle around his bowed head.

Ethel Pease

revised version appears in Peck's *Final Solution*, 1972

Ethel Pease dislikes her late shift in the Department of Electronic Security at Urban University. She seldom gets home before midnight, and in order to see her son eat breakfast she must rise by six, take the subway two miles to the Dept. of ChIld Care and stand outside the one-way window. If only she had thought to get that man's name, she might have persuaded him to marry her. She knew that any of several men might have been Warren's father. Still, it was the big one she thought about most. Married to him, she would have been able to keep Warren with her, rather than sending him to Child Care to be raised Warren Urban.

It was an old lament. All of Ethel Pease's laments are old, familiar, habituated. In the human brain there lies the potential for millions of synapses to be activated. All It takes is the movement of an idea, the minor electrical impulse along a single neuron, a simple jolt of chemical stimulation, to form a memory. With each repetition that memory becomes stronger. But, unstimulated, the brain remains a virgin plot, waiting for a chemical that never comes, waiting for that spark of current. The brain of Ethel Pease was nearly static free and powerless. Only a few repeated ideas sputtered long its pulsing surface,. Among them was her nightly lament over not having got, that, man's, name.

    Each night, sitting here listening to the forcefield shell crackling outside her office she sighed over the same collection of Ifs. It never did any good. Perhaps she knew that. But her time filled itself, and her mind worked with the only material it had stored.

    The bell rang to interrupt her reverie. Actually, her reverie ceased a moment before the bell sounded, as it did every twenty minutes, every night, out of habit, but she didn't know that. Forget cause-and-effect. The bell rang to mark her interrupted reverie, and she sighed as she climbed out of her chair.

    Time to check the equipment again. Lately, disgruntled students had begun to experiment more cleverly in their attempts to short out the field. They threw wire mesh against it, or buckets of water, anything they thought might break the curtain of flickering green power that domed Urban University and reached to the ground here at Exit East. Now, almost nightly they gathered nearby to taunt Ethel Pease, who had grown too fat of late to chase them away.

Urban University is circular. For reasons known only to five theoretical physicists in the world, a forcefield shell must be circular at the base or lose stability. It has something to do with creating a dome. The explanation lies in mathematics, not in words, but you will be able to look it up. If you like. If you can understand the math. The physicists say the explanation's "as simple as pi," and they laugh.

    The several ranks of buildings nearest the crackling mist-green shell are termed "Workring." All the manufacturing departments of the university are located in Workring. They have easy access to exit points (though no one exits). Raw materials enter through these guarded ports; manufactured goods exit. It is most efficient.

Only the faculty and students assigned to these departments dislike the location, for reasons having nothing to do with the education offered there. They dislike the noise and the stench. Not the noise of the factories but the roar of the air ducts.

Every hundred yards along the curved base of the forcefield shell there is an intake that inhales the filth of the murky atmosphere within the university. Airborn dust, debris, and careless small animals are drawn into the howling ducts, which roar like hundreds of Hoovers. The air is cleaned, purified, humidified and released once more, nearly breathable, at the center of the university in university park. The emission is silent. No one minds that.

It rises above the buildings at University Center and begins its arcing return to the ducts, On the way it accumulates sulfur, nitrous oxides, bits of carbon ash—all the effluvia of a dense industrial complex. By the time a cubic meter of purified air returns unpurified to the ducts, it contains an ounce of airborne crud and has developed a distinct character, The students who brush that air out of their weeping eyes have a definition. They say it's strong enough to gag a maggot.

It does have a tangible aroma. As the finest French perfume is to excrement, so is excrement to the air settling over Workring.

And it's Ethel Pease who keeps the dome snug enough to trap the air inside. And the students. And her own son. Because she was doing her job.

She climbed the grillwork steps to the platform overlooking the control panel. There were six dials to read, in order, left to right. Once each dial a needle pointed toward a colored arc on the perimeter of the dial. Green, green, yellow, yellow, gray . . . red. She checked the dots tattooed on her wrist, although she knew them by heart: green, green, yellow, yellow, gray, gray. Something was wrong with number six.

She plodded to the end of the platform, to No.6 rheostat, and seized the big wheel with both hands. She turned it slowly until the number 6 needle moved into the gray, then she paused to listen.

She may have noticed a change in the field. Perhaps not. It still crackled outside, and above, and around her station. Now all the needles pointed exactly where they should.

Esther slumped down the grillwork steps, sighing. How did people get so old so fast? Every time she makes this particular descent she ponders the same question. Its frequent recurrence had something to do with the effect of gravity on her brain. Nearly forty, came the thought. All her girlish plans long since abandoned. She had hoped to go to graduate school but something had gone wrong. Twenty-eight years ago—that wasn't her calculation; she thought "once"—she had been among the first to take Retardo. It hadn't worked so well then, or perhaps it hadn't worked on someone already eleven years old. In either case, it hadn't worked. During her senior year, after eight faithful years on the drug, her breasts began to develop.

She took to skipping hygiene class. Why take pill? It wasn't fulfilling its office. And then she grew proud of her sprouting pubic hair and the swelling visible under her blouse.

Men noticed. How could a young girl completely inexperienced fend off the men at holiday parties? Especially the big one, the professor from the Foundry Dept. or Welding or somewhere important.

Along came Warren. And the nice doctors at the . . . the white place where they delivered the babies . . . those doctors fixed her so there would be no more babies. Off Retardo, she had no chance of further schooling. The B.S. was all, for her. She knew her colors and numbers. They could trust her to be faithful in her work, or never see Warren again.

She took the whistling tea kettle off the coil. She might have time for a cup of tea before the bell rang and made her check the dials. It was not a bad job, after all: green, green, yellow, yellow, gray, gray.

Gantlet

first published in *Orbit 10*, 1972

Jack Brens thumbed the ID sensor and waited for the sealed car doors to open. He'd stayed too long in his office, hoping to avoid conversation with the other commuters, and had been forced to trot through the fetid station. The doors slit open. He ducked in and sucked gratefully at the cool air inside, then scrubbed his damp palms along his thighs and surveyed the car. Rivulets of sweat ran down the small of his back. He stretched his lips into the parody of a confident smile.

Most of the passengers sat strapped in. A few feigned sleep, others tried to concentrate on the stiff-dried facsheets that rattled in their hands. Lances of light fell diagonally through the gloom; some of the boiler plate welded over the windows had cracked under the twice-daily barrage.

Brens bit the tip of his tongue to remind himself to call Co-op Maintenance when he got home. Today the train was his responsibility—one day out of one hundred; one day out of twenty work weeks. Flaws uncorrected today could burn him tomorrow, though the responsibility would then shift to someone else. To whom?

Karras. Tomorrow Karras had Window Seat.

Brens nodded to several of the gray-haired passengers who greeted him.

"Hey, Brens. How's it going?"

"Hello, Mr. Brens."

"Go get'em, Jack."

He strode down the aisle through the aura of acrid fear marking the ninety-odd men huddled in their seats. A few of the commuters had already pulled down their individual smoking bells from the overhead rack. Although the rules forbade smoking till the train got underway, Brens understood their anxiety too well to make a point of it.

Only Karras sat at the front. The seats beside and behind him were empty.

"Thought you weren't coming and I might have to take her out myself," Karras said. "But my turn tomorrow."

Brens nodded and slipped into the engineer's seat. While he familiarized himself with the instrument console, he felt Karras peering past him at the window. Lights in the station tunnel faded and the darkness outside made the window a temporary mirror. Brens glanced at it once to see the split image of Karras reflected in the inner and outer layers of the bulletproof glass: four bulging eyes, a pair of glistening bald scalps wobbling in and out of focus.

The start buzzer sounded.

He checked the interior mirror. Only two empty seats, at the front of course. He'd heard of no resignations from the Co-op and therefore assumed that the men who should have occupied those seats were ill. It took something serious to make a man miss his scheduled car and incur the fine of a full day's salary.

The train thrummed to life. Lights flared, the fans whined toward full thrust, and the car danced unsteadily forward as it wobbled and ballooned onto its cushion of air. Brens concentrated on keeping his hovering hands near the throttle override.

"You really sweat this thing, don't you?" Karras said. "Relax. Enjoy the view, unless you think you're really playing engineer."

Brens tried to ignore him. It was true that the train was almost totally automatic. Yet the man who drew window seat did have certain responsibilities, functions to perform, and little time to waste. No time until the train was safely beyond the third circle—past Cityend, past Opensky, past Workring. And after that, an easy thirty miles home.

Brens pictured the city above them as the train bored its way through the subterranean darkness, pushing it back with a fan of brilliant light. City stretched for thirty blocks from center in this direction and then met the wall of defenses separating City from Opensky. The whole area of City was unified now, finally—buildings joined and sealed against the filth of the air outside that massive, nearly self-sufficient hive. Escalators up and down, beltways back and forth, interior temperature and pollution kept at an acceptable level. It was almost pleasant.

It was heaven, compared to Opensky. Surrounding and continually threatening City lay the ring of Opensky and its incredible masses of people. Brens hadn't been there for years, not since driving though on this way to work had become impossibly time-consuming and dangerous. Twenty years ago he had been one of the last lucky ones, picked out by Welfare Control as "salvageable." These days, no one left Opensky. For that matter, no one with good sense entered.

He could vaguely recall seeing single-family dwellings there, whether his wife, Hazel, believed that claim or not. Vivid in memory was the single-family room he had shared with his parents and grandfather. He could even remember the first O-peddlers to appear on Sheridan Street. Huge, brawny men with green O-tanks strapped to their back, they joked with the clamoring children who tugged at their sleeves and tried to beg a lungful of straight O for the high it was rumored to induce. But the peddlers dealt at first only with asthmatics and early-stage emphysemics who gathered on muggy afternoons to suck their metered dollar's worth from the grimy rubber face looped over the peddler's arm. All that, before each family had a private bubble hooked directly to the City metering system.

Brens had no idea what life in Opensky was like now, except what he could gather from the statistics that crossed his desk in Welfare Control. Those figures meant little enough: so many schools to maintain, dole centers to keep stocked and guarded, restraint aides needed for various playgrounds . . . he converted City budget figures to percentages corresponding to the requests of fieldmen in Opensky, then doled out appropriate portions to each. He hadn't spoken to a fieldman in nearly a year. But he assumed it couldn't be pleasant there.

Welfare Control had recently disbanded and reassigned to wall duty all Riot Suppression teams. The object now was no longer to suppress, a futile plan, but to contain. What went on in Opensky was the 'Skyers' own business, so long as they didn't try to enter City.

So. Six miles through Opensky surrounding City to Workring, three miles of Workring itself, where the 'Skyers kept the furnaces bellowing and City industry alive. But that part of the trip wouldn't be too bad. Only responsible 'Skyers were allowed to enter Workring, and most stuck to their jobs or risked having their thumbprints erased from the sensors at each Opensky exit gate. Such strict control had seemed harsh, at first, but Brens knew it was necessary. Rampant sabotage in Workring had made it so. The 'Skyers who chose to work had controlled access to and from Workring. And those who chose not to work, well, that was their choice. They could occupy themselves somehow. Each year Welfare Control authorized more and more playgrounds in Opensky, and the public school gymnasiums and bowling alleys were open to anyone under fifty with no worse than a moderate arrest record.

Beyond Workring lay the commuter residential area. A few miles of high-rise suburbs, for secretaries and apprentice managerial staff, merging suddenly with the sprawling redevelopment apartment blocks, and then real country. To Brens the commuter line seemed a barometer of social responsibility: the greater one's worth to the City, the farther away one could afford to live. Brens and his wife had moved for the last time only a year ago, to the end of the trainpad, thirty miles out. They owned a small square of yellowed grass and two dwarf apple trees that would not bear. It was . . .

He shook off his daydreaming and focused on the darkness rushing toward them. As their speed increased, he paradoxically lost the sense of motion conveyed by the lurching start and lumbering underground passage. Greater speed increased the compression pad below as air entered the trains howling scoops and whooshed through the ducts down the car sides. Cityend lay moments ahead.

Brens concentrated on one of the few tasks not yet automated. At Cityend, and on the train's emergence from the tunnel, lay his real task. Three times in the past month 'Skyers had sought to breach City defenses through the tunnel itself.

Only Karras, who now sat hunched forward in anticipation, would enjoy that possibility. Because Karras was sick. The man seemed to look forward to his turn in Window Seat, not only for the sights all the other commuters in the Co-op hoped to avoid or ignore, but also for the possible opportunity of turning loose the train's newly installed firepower.

"One of these days they're going to make a big try," Karras said. He bounced in his seat. "They'd all give an arm to break into City, just to camp in the corridors. Now, if it was me out there, I'd be figuring a way to bust into the Suburbs. But them? All they know is destroy. Besides, you think they'll take it lying down that we raised the O-tax? Forget it! They're out there waiting, and we both know it. That's why you ought to check all the gear we've got. Never know when—"

"Later, Karras! There it is." Brens felt his chest tighten as the distant circle of light swept toward them—tunnel exit, Cityend. His forearms tensed and he glared at the instruments, waiting for the possibility that he might have to override the controls and slam the train to a stop. But a green light flashed ahead. The circle of sky brightened as the approaching train tripped the switch that cut off the spray of mist at the tunnel exit. And with that mist fading, the barrier of twenty thousand volts that crackled between the exit uprights faded also. For the next few moments, while the train snaked its way into Opensky, City was potentially vulnerable.

Brens stared even harder at the opening but saw nothing. The car flashed out into gray twilight, and he relaxed. But instinct, or a random impulse, drew his eyes to the train's exterior mirrors. And then he saw them: a shapeless huddle of bodies pouring into the tunnel back toward City. He hit a series of studs on the console and braced himself for the jolt.

There it was.

A murmur swept the crowded car behind him, but he ignored it and stared straight ahead.

"What the hell was it?" Karras said. "I didn't see a thing."

"'Skyers. They were waiting, I guess, till the first car passed. They must have figured no one would see them that way."

"I don't mean *who*. I mean, what did you use? I didn't hear the fifties."

"For a man who's taking the run tomorrow, you don't keep up very well. Nothing fancy, none of the noise and flash some people get their kicks from. I just popped speed breaks on the last three cars."

"In the tunnel? My God! Must have wiped them all the way out the tunnel walls, like a squeegee. Who figured that one?"

"This morning's Co-op bulletin suggested it, remember?"

Karras sulked. "I've got better things to do than read every word those guys put out. They must spend all day dictating memos. We got a real bunch of clods running things this quarter."

"Why don't you volunteer?"

"I give them my four days' pay a month. That's it!"

Brens silently agreed. No one enjoyed keeping the Co-op alive. No one really knew how. And that was one of the major problems associated with having amateurs in charge: it's

Gantlet

a hell of a way to run a railroad. But the only way, since the line itself had declared bankruptcy, and both city and state governments refused to take over. If it hadn't been for the Co-op, City would have died, a festering ulcer in the cancer of Opensky.

Opensky whirled past them now. Along the embankment on both sides, legs dangled a decorative fringe. People sat atop the pilings and hurled debris at the speeding stainless steel cars. Their accuracy had always amazed Brens. Even as he willed himself rigid, he flinched at the eggs, rocks, bottles, and assorted garbage that clattered and smeared across the window.

"Look at those sonsabitches throw, would you?" Karras bounced in his seat again. "You ever try and figure what kind of lead time you need to hit something moving as fast as we are?"

Brens shook his head. "I guess they're used to it."

"Why not? What else they got to do but practice?"

Behind them, gunfire crackled and bullets pattered along the boiler plate. Many of the commuters ducked at the opening burst.

"Look at them back there." Karras pointed down the aisle. "Scarred blue, every one of them. I know this psychologist who's got a way to calm things down, he says. He had this idea to paint bull's-eyes on the sides of the cars, below the window. Did I tell you about it? He figures it'll work two or three ways."

"Yeah, invite more gunfire"

"No, if the snipers hit the bull's-eyes, there's less chance of somebody getting tagged through a crack in the boiler plate. Two, maybe they'll quit firing at all, when they see we don't give a suck of sky about it. Or Three, he says, even if they keep it up, it gives them something to do, sort of channels their aggression. If they take it out on the trains, maybe they'll ease up on City. What do you think?

"Wouldn't it make more sense to disarm them? Or figure a way to get new cars for the trains? We can't keep patching these old crates forever. The last thing we need right now is to make us more of a target than we already are."

"Okay? Have it your way. Only, I was thinking . . ."

Brens tuned him out and squinted at the last molten sliver of setting sun. Its rays lit rainbows through the streaked eggs washing slowly across the window in the slipstream. The mess coagulated and darkened as airblown particles of ash settled in it and crusted over. When he could stand it no longer, Brens flipped on the wipers and watched the clotted slime smear across the glass. But some of it scrubbed loose to flip back alongside the speeding train.

The people were still out there. If he looked carefully straight ahead, their presence became a mere shadow at the edges of the channel through which he watched the trainpad reeling toward him. Though he doubted any eye would catch his long enough to matter, he avoided the faces. There was always the slight chance that he might recognize one of them. There were survivors. Twenty years wasn't so long a time. Twenty years go he had watched the trains from an embankment like these.

Now the train swooped upward to ride its cushion of air along the raised pad, level with second-story windows on each side. Blurred faces stared from those windows, here disembodied, there resting on a cupped hand and arm propped on a window ledge. The exterior mirrors showed him faces ducking away from the gust of gritty wind fanning out behind the train and from the debris lifted whirling in the grimy evening air. He tried to picture the pattern left by the train's passage—dust settling out of the whirlwind like the parentheses of iron filings around a magnet tip.

A few of the faces wore respirators or simple, and useless, cotton masks. Many didn't bother to draw back but hung exposed to the breeze that the train was stirring up. And now, as on each of his previous rare turns at the window seat, Brens had the impulse to slow the train, to let the wind die down and diminish behind them, out of what he himself considered misplaced sympathy for the 'Skyers, who seemed to enjoy the excitement of the train's glistening passage. It tempered the boredom of their day.

". . . right about here the six-thirty had the explosion. Five months ago. Remember?"

"What?"

"Explosion. Some kids got hold of detonator caps and strung them on wires swinging from a tree. When the train hit them, they cracked the window all to hell. Could have hurt somebody. But the crews came out and burned down all the trees along the right of way. Little bastards won't pull that one again."

Brens nodded. There was one of the armored repair vans ahead, on a siding under the overhanging stone lip of the embankment. The train rose even higher to cross the river which formed the Opensky-Workring boundary. They were riding securely in the concave shell of the bridge. On the river below, a cat, or dog—hard to tell at this distance—picked its cautious way across the crusted algae which nearly covered the stream. The center of the turgid river steamed a molten beige, and upriver a short way, brilliant patches of green marked the mouth of the main Workring spillway.

At the far end of the bridge, a group of children scrambled out of the trough of the trainbed to hang over the side.

"Hey! Hit the lasers. Singe their butts for them." Karras ricked in his seat.

"Shut up for a minute, can't you? They're out of the way."

"Why the attitude? Can't you take a joke? Besides, you know they're sneaking into Workring to steal something. You saying we ought to let them get away with it?"

"I'm just telling you to shut up. I'm tired, that's all. Leave it at that."

"Sure. Big deal. Tired! But tomorrow the window seat's mine. So don't come sucking around for a look then, understand?"

"It's a promise."

Sulfurous clouds hung in the air, and Brens checked the car's interior pollution level. It was a safe 18, as he might have guessed. But the sight of buildings tarnished green, of bricks flaking and molting on every factory wall, always depressed him. The ride home was worse than the trip into City. Permissive hours ran from five to eight, when pollution controls were lifted. He knew the theory: evening air was more susceptible to condensation because of the temperature drop, and spraying pollutants into the night sky might actually bring on a cleansing rain. He also knew the practical considerations involved: twenty-four-hour control would almost certainly drive industry away. Compromise was essential, if City was to survive.

It would be good to get home.

The train swung into its gently curving descent toward Workring exit, and Brens instinctively clasped the seat arms as the seat pivoted on its gimbals. At the foot of the curve he saw the barricade. Something piled on the pad.

Not for an instant did he doubt what he saw. He lunged at the power override but stopped himself in time. Dropping to the pad now, in mid-curve, might tip the train or let it slide off the pad onto the potholed and eroded right of way where the uneven terrain offered no stable life base for getting underway again.

"Ahead of you! On the tracks!" Karras reached for the controls, but Brens caught him with a straight-arm and slammed him to the floor. He concentrated on the roadbed flashing toward them. At the last instant, as the curve modified and tilted toward level, he popped all speedbreaks and snatched the main circuit breaker loose.

From the sides of the cars vertical panels hissed out on their hydraulic pushrods to form baffles against the slipstream, and the train slammed to the pad. Tractor gear whined in protest, the shriek nearly drowning out the dying whirr of compressor fans, and the train shuddered to a stop.

Inside, lights dimmed and flickered. Voices rose in the darkness amid noise of men struggling to their feet.

Brens depressed the circuit breaker and hit the emergency call switch overhead. "Hold it!" he shouted. "Quiet down, please! There's something on the pad, and I had to stop. Just keep calm. I've signaled for the work crews, and they'll be here any minute."

He ignored the passengers and focused his attention on the window. The barricade lay no more than twenty feet ahead, rusted castings and discarded mold shells heaped on the roadbed. The jumbled pile seemed ablaze in the flickering red light from the emergency beacons rotating atop the train cars. Behind the barricade and along the right of way, faceless huddled forms rose erect in the demonic light and stood motionless, simply staring at the train. The stroboscopic light sweeping over them made each face a swarm of moving, melting shadows. Brens fired a preliminary burst from the fifties atop the first car, then switched them to automatic, but . . . no reaction. The watching forms stood like statues.

"They must know," Karras said. He stood beside Brens and massaged his bruised shoulder. "Look. None of them moving."

Then one of the watchers broke and charged toward the car, waving a club. He managed two strides before the fifties homed on his movement and opened up. A quick chatter from overhead and the man collapsed. He hurled the club as he dropped and the fifties efficiently followed its arc through the air with homed fire that made it dance in a shower of flashing sparks. It splintered to shreds before it hit the ground.

The other watchers stood motionless.

Brens stared at them a long moment before he could define what puzzled him about their appearance: none of them wore respirators. Were they trying to commit suicide? And why this useless attack?

His eyes had grown accustomed to the flickering light and he scanned the mob. Young faces and old, mostly men but a few women scattered among them, all shades of color, united in appearance only by their clothing. Workring 'Skyers in leather aprons, thick-soled shoes, probably escapees from a nearby factory. He flinched as one of them nodded slightly.

Surely they couldn't see him through the window. The nod grew more violent, and then he realized that the man was coughing. Paroxysms seized the man as he threw his hands to his mouth and bent forward helplessly. It was enough. The fifties chattered once more, and he fell.

"But what do they get out of it?" He turned his bewilderment to Karras.

"Who can tell? They're nuts, all of them. Malcontents, or even anarchists. Mainly stupid, I'd say. Like the way they try and break into City. Even if they threw us out, they wouldn't know squat about what to do next. Picture one of them sitting in your office. At your desk."

"I don't mean that. If they stop us from getting through, who takes care of them? We feed them, run their schools, bury them. I don't understand what they think all this will accomplish."

"Listen! The crew's coming. They'll give 'em what for!"

A siren keened its rise and fall from the dimming twilight ahead, but still the watchers stood frozen. When the siren changed to a blatting klaxon, Brens switched the fifties back on manual to safeguard the approaching repair car. The mob melted away at the same signal. They were there, and then they were gone. They dropped from sight along the pad edge and blended into the shadows.

The work crew's crane hoisted the castings off the pad and dropped them on the right of way shoulder. In a few minutes they had finished. Green lights flashed the all-clear, and the repair van sped away again.

Passing the Workring exit guards, Brens made a mental note to warn the Co-op. If the 'Skyers were growing bold enough to show open rebellion within the security of Workring, the exit guards had better be augmented. Even Suburbs might not be safe any longer. At thirty miles distance, he wasn't really concerned for his own home, but some of the commuters lived dangerously close to Workring.

He watched in the exterior mirror. The rear car detached itself and swung out onto a siding where it dropped to a halt while the body of the train went on. Every two miles, the scene repeated itself. Cars dropped off singly to await morning reassembly. Brens had often felt a strange sort of envy for the commuters who lived closer in: they never had the lead window seat on the way out of City. Responsibility for the whole train devolved on them only for short stretches, only on the way in.

But that was fair, he reminded himself. He lived the farthest out. With privilege go obligations. And he was through, for another twenty weeks, his obligations met.

At the station, he faxed his report to the Co-op office and trotted outside to meet Hazel. The other wives had driven away. Only his carryall sat idling at the platform edge. He knew he ought to look forward to relaxing at home, but the trip itself still preyed on his mind unaccountably. He felt irritation at his inability to put the 'Skyers out of his thoughts. His whole day was spent working for their benefit; his evenings ought to be his own.

He looked back toward City, but saw nothing in the smog-covered bowl at the foot of the hills that stretched away to the east. Hazel smiled and waved.

He grinned in answer. He could predict her reaction when she heard what he'd been through: a touch of wifely fear and concern for him, and that always made her more affectionate. Almost a hero's welcome. After all, he had acquitted himself well. A safe arrival, only a few minutes late, no injuries or major problems. And he wouldn't draw window seat again for another several months. It was good to be home.

Deliveryman

first published in *Amazing Science Fiction Stories*, September 1975

In the pale red light of the briefing room Lee Roma's fingernails took on an eerie sheen. Only moments before he had swallowed two uppers, and now the sights and sounds of the room floated behind a mist as his own reflexes outraced sensory input. Coates' droning voice slowed to a bass growl. Roma recognized distortion—his own time sense, grown subjectively fleet. He tried to recall the "real" sound of Coates' whining tenor but couldn't. Real is what you make it. He focused on his glistening pink fingernails and listened.

"... thing matters. Only one. Get the load through. Clear?"

Muttered assent.

"What?" Coates shouted. "I can't hear you."

"*Yessir!*" Ten voices in unison. Ten men clad only in sandals and trunks.

Coates nodded. "Check linkups."

Like the others, in silent pantomime, Roma went through the ritual with automatic hands: glucose and stimulant receptor tubes hanging free on his groin; EKG stud uncapped; throat mike strapped tight around his neck (it rode on the quick beat of his pulse); EEG stud uncapped. His moist palm touched crotch, chest, throat, forehead, in a parody of salaam.

And there were his nails again, hovering before his eyes in the hell-lit room.

"Roma! You with us or not?"

"Sir!"

"Educated nitwits." Coates talked to the ceiling in mock despair. "Why do I get them all?"

Several chuckles in the room; and Roma bit back an answer. A few hours more and it would be over. No more of Coates' riding him, no more of the constant needling: "Big deal, Roma. College man. What do we do now? Bow down and kiss your feet? Why's a guy like you want to be a deliveryman?" Always the same refrain. Singled out. One man, in a class of ten—the brunt of Coates' practiced sarcasm. But in a few hours that would be done with, over. Make this run, and then forget that he'd ever met Coates.

"All right. Last thing now. I'll be riding with you all the way. Don't forget it. I've got the switch in my hand. One of you screws up, and that's the end. If you even *think* about leaving the Crawler, I'll hit the switch sure as hell. One thing matters to you: get this load through. One thing matters to me: the 'Skyers don't get one of the crawlers." Coates paused.

Closing his eyes, Roma felt the weight of Coates' stare and waited for the verbal attack—general harangue to the class, made specific for Roma. It never came.

"Well?" Coates posed with folded arms. "What are you waiting for? Want an escort? Man 'em." He spun and walked through the archway back into Central.

Roma pushed past two men hesitating at the door and broke into a trot down the darkened tunnel. The sooner there, the sooner done.

Ten Crawlers stood ranked in the exit bay, number ten—Roma's—farthest from the portal. Even as he palmed the lock and watched the hatch swing open he knew it was intentional. One more of Coates' little games. Put Roma in his place, make him last to churn through the exit port. Last, and therefore the most exposed.

The first Crawler out was safe enough—departure unscheduled, destination unknown. By the time ten passed though the port into the night, anyone lying in ambush would be more than ready to attack. Roma shrugged and shook his arms limp to relax. He could handle it.

The heated swivel chair caressed Roma's bare skin as he settled into it, reshaping itself to his contours, becoming one with him. He smiled at the sensuality of the welcome. He reached down to activate the thermite charge in the base of the chair, then plugged in. EEG, mike jack, EKG, glucose and stimulant—and he was one with the Crawler, technically a cybernaut, in the jargon a "deliveryman."

"Not man. *Boy.* That's the word," Coates always said. At the beginning of every training session, as each candidate plugged into the jacks of the Crawler simulator. "*Boy.* One mistake and I hit the thermite switch. Don't forget it. You're mine, till I say otherwise."

"I won't forget it," Roma muttered.

"Talking to me, Boy?" Coates voice rasped in his ears. "Have you got something to say?"

"No sir."

"You look pretty nervous, you know that? Your EEG's got a flutter in the Alpha. Why do you suppose that is?"

"Uppers, sir. They do it to me."

"All right. Let's pretend that's true. But if you get scared, *Boy*, let me know. We can recall you and send out a man."

Roma refused to be baited. He flipped on the viewer and checked 360 degrees. All cameras working. He saw the other nine Crawlers shuddering before him at idle. Internal check showed the cargo compartment hatch secured, all comm and defense systems in the green. He dropped his right hand into the control socket in the chair arm, and relaxed.

"Go!"

At Coates' shout the exit iris cycled and the first Crawler lurched out into the darkness.

"Fields! You're next. Move it!"

Number two churned forward on its treads, and the remaining eight closed the gap. As they inched forward into the night, Roma held a close interval on number nine and waited tensed for Coates' inevitable criticism.

The Crawler cabin crackled with blue static as it passed through the charged exit field, and then—

"Left! Left! Left! Where the hell you going, Roma? Left, I said."

Treads bit through the rubble piled outside and the Crawler swung heavily left to mount a small incline of brick and crumbled plaster. His night vision prepared by the red lights of the briefing room, Roma ran a quick check of the narrow street ahead of him. No one. Empty. None of the ambushers he'd feared. His hand moved automatically, controlling direction and speed with a gimbal-mounted stick and twist-throttle combination. Almost helicopter controls, minus the vertical component. Just like the simulator. Like the hundreds of mock deliveries he had made during three months of incessant study, and practice, and drill. In his feet he felt the Crawler's treads grind inexorably over the trash-cluttered street. Through the cab's audio he heard the roar of his own passage. And while he was one with the Crawler, Coates was nearly one with him.

"Calmer now, Roma? Think it's a piece of cake, do you? You're looking good on the gauges. But we'll fix that. Let me give you a route. Set your GPS."

"Ready to copy, sir." Roma's free hand hovered over a keyboard in the left chairarm.

"Parkway to 35th, Wilton Bridge to the Armory, Bariss Street to 70th, 70th to Renault. Got it?"

"Renault? But that's—"

"I know where it is, *Boy*. Do you? I've got nine other incompetents on the board right now. I can't coddle you. Do you copy?"

"Sir."

"I'm watching. Go to it."

On the Crawler's instrument console a map of the city glowed lime green, overlaid now with a pink line marking the route Roma had punched in. In his mind's eye he saw the entire city laid out with hard-edged clarity, a grid bisected by the diagonal twist of river squirming its way northeast to southwest. His route lay across the river toward the most distant corner of the mental map he now reviewed. It passed from the tower complex of City, through the exit port into the danger of Opensky, through Opensky into Workring, and nearly to Suburbs. Almost fifteen miles, a full radius of the built-up area surrounding City itself. Fifteen miles in a vehicle with a top speed of ten mph. A check of the clock

Deliveryman

confirmed his fears. Another hour of darkness at most; dawn would catch him well short of 70th and Renault, in the open, exposed to any attack the 'Skyers might mount.

He swung right onto the Parkway and opened the throttle. Full speed was impossible; he didn't dare outrun his infra red lights and heat sensors. But the more distance he could cover now, the less time he had to risk in daylight. The Parkway was cluttered with abandoned vehicles, some of them temporary homes at one time but empty since the chaos. He slewed around large obstacles, ran over, or through, smaller ones.

In a moment his actions had grown automatic, the result of repeated sessions in the simulator. His mind ticked over the alphabetical list of drop-points until he reached "Renault and 70th." *Dole center; former bank; two permanent volunteer staff; class one zone—high risk drop-point.*

Coates had given him a beauty, first trip out of City. Okay. He could handle it. He shook his head—his neck ached from tension—and felt drops of perspiration sprinkle his bare arms. *Sweating?* He thumbed the temperature control lower and tried to relax. Nearly 0500. By now his parents would be having breakfast, safe in City towers. Where Roma could have stayed—*should* have stayed, his mother would say . . .

A three-room luxury apartment, but no more than the Romas' eminence deserved: Baird Roma, PhD (Chemistry), Director City Watersupply; Eileen Cohn-Roma, MD (Obstet), PhD (Microbiology), Co-Director PopPlanning; Lee Roma, BS (Ecosystems), unemployed. And that was the cause of their daily breakfast argument.

"Did you talk to Delivery?" Lee tried to make his question sound casual and unconcerned, but his mother's indrawn breath defined his failure.

"I meant to," his father said. "I just didn't get the chance." He scooped out a spoonful of soft-boiled egg and bent low to hide his lie.

"When will you get the chance? How long can it take?" His mother pushed back from the table and nearly upset her chair. "Will you stop it! Both of you. I'm sick to death of this fencing. Every morning the same thing. You first." She gestured at Baird. "Tell him the truth. We *won't* pull any strings to get him into Delivery, and that's the end of it."

Baird nodded with resignation. "Your mother's right, Lee. You know what the competition's like. Three, sometimes four men a day try to run the maze through Opensky. On foot! And when one of them makes it inside City, he's earned the right to a job. Why should you expect preferential treatment?"

"I don't. You know that. But what's left for me? I'm inside already. No one's going to let me out to try the maze, so what's left?"

"A *responsible* job." His mother glared at him, fighting back tears of anger and frustration. "Deliveryman! With your education? It's absurd! And that's not a proud mother speaking, either. You know that. You both know that. But you've seen the extrapolations. A few months, a year at the most, and we'll have Opensky pacified. We'll start the schools running again. We'll—"

"Uh-huh. I know the whole song and dance." Lee slumped in his chair, angry at his own pouting but sullen nevertheless. Whichever way he turned he faced a blank wall.

"That's enough!" Baird slammed his spoon to the table. "Apologize, and right now. Your mother is only concerned for you, and all we hear is sarcasm."

Flushed, Lee nodded. "You're right. I'm sorry. I really am. But you said we'd 'discuss' it. Will you listen to me?" He took their reluctant nods as a minor victory, then hesitated before beginning.

It wasn't a long speech, but it was carefully rehearsed. For weeks he had been sifting and winnowing, separating chaff from wheat, sorting and refining his arguments to condense them within the most logical framework he could devise. He claimed an expertise his parents lacked. They were specialists, the very sort in whom the only hope for City lay. But Lee was not. A generalist, he had tried synthesizing several disciplines. His formal course of study had been designated "Ecosystems." It might better be termed "the City." To his mind and imagination, City was alive, though moribund. It could be brought back to life.

"That's what *I've* been saying," his mother interrupted. "In PopPlanning you could—"

"Mother? Please."

Baird silenced her with a frown.

At the risk of boring them but determined to follow a single thread to the end, Lee summarized the chaos; collapse of the school system, of civil order, of public services, leading finally to mass riots and looting. There had been rumors of cannibalism. Evidence replaced the rumors; City tightened security. And much of the problem—to Lee's mind—stemmed from simple facts of geography.

"Take a look out the window," he said. "You'll see what I

mean. Oh, I know. You'll tell me you look every day, but you don't *see* it. Here we are, safe in City, all the managerial class. Circling City, the slums we euphemize as 'Opensky.' Open! There's nothing open about it: surrounded by the guarded factories in Workring, locked out of City—no wonder the 'Skyers riot. Money and power on one hand, but out of their reach. Jobs on the other hand, but not enough for everyone. And beyond Workring, Suburbs! Luxury. *Real* open spaces—"

"Nonsense," his mother snapped. "That old commuter class is gone, and you know it. Take us. Didn't we move back? Aren't we here now, where our responsibilities lie? Suburbs are a myth. Only the farms and agronomy stations—"

"I know that. So do you. What about the 'Skyers? So long as they think there's a paradise out beyond Workring, of course they'll rebel. My God! You're treating them like animals. We need to break down these barriers, not defend or redefine them."

Baird looked at his watch in an obvious attempt to cut off the argument. "Can we get to the end? How will your joining Delivery change anything? Isn't that the question?"

"It may not." As much as he hated the admission, Lee felt compelled to make it. His argument hinged on a truth he didn't want tainted by any deceit, not even one necessary to achieving his goal. Means and ends have to match. "But I think this is true. I may be the only one in City who really sees the problem. Not a solution, not yet, but the problem itself. City's the bullseye in a target. All those concentric rings out there have to merge, meld, blend together. I *think* that's true. If I can get outside, really participate, *feel* Opensky and what it's like—maybe I'll *know*."

Deliveryman

Eileen shook her head. "That's too facile. Nearly everyone now in Delivery came from Opensky, and you don't see any of them trying to get back outside City. They're—"

"Should I be a climber because they are? I know what security's like. It's farce, artifice. There's no security for us till it's available for the 'Skyers, too."

The argument droned on. And on. Only his final threat, saved for a desperate last attempt, had any effect: "I will go out. That's all there is. Now, if you can get me a chance to work in delivery, fine. I'll go out legally. If not . . ." He let the implication hang in the tense air between them.

And a week later, with all the bad grace she could muster, Eileen told him it was arranged: Lee Roma, BS, a member of the new Delivery training class.

He moved out of his parents' apartment and into ten-man, two-room quarters, deep in the bowels of City. And into the hands of Coates.

"Report!"

Roma ran a quick exterior check before answering. "All clear. No problems. Now approaching Wilton Bridge."

"No problems? Pretty cocky, aren't you? Let me pose one. Say you cross the bridge, and there's a human barricade. Then what?"

Roma hesitated. He had the answer all right, the book solution, but it didn't come easily to his tongue.

"Well, *Boy*. Let's have it."

"Get the load through."

"I know that, you nit! How?"

Through clenched teeth, Roma snapped back, "Any way!"

"Will you do it? Through them? Over them, if you have to?"

"If I have to."

"We'll see. Get set. A report just came in from the Armory drop-point. 'Skyers massing two blocks from the bridge. An ugly crowd. Be ready."

"Sir."

The Crawler rumbled onto the bridge. Holes gaped in the twisted metal railing to his right. In two places the concrete flooring had heaved and buckled. Massive slabs leaned against each other, pairs of mammoth playing cards propped tent-like on a huge tabletop. Roma swung right around the first obstruction, his outside tread grating along the retaining barrier over the river. Through the starboard cameras he saw only open water beneath. The stick grew mushy in his hands. The Crawler hung teetering a breathless moment, then lurched left onto solid footing.

The second obstruction was smaller. The Crawler climbed it and dropped slowly down the far incline. Roma twisted the throttle and thundered toward the west bank.

He flinched at the noise of his progress. Running with infra red lights gave him partial security, but the engine's roar marked his location for anyone within a block or two. With a crowd gathering ahead, speed became more important than stealth.

A futile log barricade at the west end of the bridge splintered to shreds under the Crawler's weight. Roma checked defense systems again, more from nervousness than need, and watched the hulking armory loom at him out of the dark. It was an inky silhouette against a sky brightening from dead black to dawn blue. A run to the Armory drop-point would end here. Roma's run stretched on miles farther.

Heat sensors picked up the crowd before Roma saw them.

He switched his console map to closeup and focused on a four-block square. A shifting clot of white marked the mass of bodies concealed beside the Armory. The white smear lay across the dotted pink line of his route.

He hesitated, then locked his right tread, and the Crawler spun sharply off the street. It tore through a flimsy electrified fence and lumbered along the west riverbank. He knew there must be a way through the Armory grounds and around the building on the near side. He could avoid the massed crowd. Viewers showed him little but vague shadows ahead, river to the right, the massive shape of buildings to his left. No matter what shortcut he took the 'Skyers would hear the Crawler. Stealth was impossible now. He snapped on the carbon arc mounted on the Crawler's bow, and in the glaring white path ahead he saw obstruction. A pile of crates, cartons of some sort, lay between him and the cross street beyond the Armory lot. He opened the throttle and slammed through the stacked boxes. His viewers became kaleidoscopes of shifting shapes as the crates flipped back over the Crawler in a shower of shattered fragments. The Crawler slammed into a solid barrier. Hesitated. The engine screamed in protest, and then with a tearing sound it was through. And onto the pavement.

He swung left and crept toward the shifting white blob on his console map. A block to Bariss Street. At full power he reached the intersection mere seconds ahead of the ambushers. Now he could see them on the viewers—scores of them, shadows in the darkness boiling out of buildings and pouring toward him.

A skidding right turn and he was onto Bariss. He'd made it! Excitement surged through him as he activated the skirt fans and watched dust and debris whirl high in the air around him. Rushing forms nearest the Crawler were seized by a giant hand and hurled off their feet; the tornado he rode in swept them away like so many rag dolls caught before the wind.

Made it! Without harming anyone. His way. And the hell with Coates. His left hand pounded exultant rhythms on the chairarm. He shut down the fans and smiled at his success.

"Roma? What are you doing?" Coates sounded pained.

"On Bariss, proceeding toward 70th. I avoided the ambush." Lee couldn't keep the note of triumph out of his voice.

"I know that. Want to hear what else I know? I taped it, not two minutes ago. Listen."

A new voice entered the cabin, tense and angry. "Central! Central! What's going on? There's a Crawler outside the Armory drop-point, smashing through the storage yard. He's just about . . . There! He did it! Tore the billy-blue-hell out of the clothing dump. It's not bad enough we've got to mount guards . . . Oh God! Now he smashed through the fence! Is that you at Central, Coates? You tell that idiot we'll be two days securing this place. And if I found out who it was, I'll . . ."

"Heard enough, Roma?" Coates interrupted the taped complaint. "I gave you a route to follow. You think I was kidding? Or did you think at all?"

"I'll get the load through," Roma barked. "And they won't get the Crawler. The rest of it's up to me. You said so yourself."

"And you're the smart one of the bunch. Damn! Okay, *Boy*. We'll talk about it later."

From their first meeting on, Coates and Roma disagreed about means.

"If a Deliveryman gets through, no harming to anyone, that's his job too, isn't it?"

Coates faced the class and shook his head. "Always an argument, Roma. I might have known. All right. Say you can do that. Good. But, if it comes down to 'Skyers or your load, you'd going to have to react."

"I can decide when it happens, sir."

"Not decide, dammit! React! If you've got this notion you can talk a mob out of cutting your throat, you're plain nuts. Ask the others. They've been there. They know."

Roma's nine classmates nodded, and their smugness—their assumption of superiority—only strengthened his determination.

"All right. So I haven't been out there yet. But you make the 'Skyers sound like a bunch of animals. If you'd treat them—"

Coates interrupted. "Not animals. No one ever said that. That's your word. They're people, right enough, but gone crazy. Not all of them. That's why there's still hope, because we can do something for most of them, *if* the loads get through. Understand that?"

"Sir."

"One more time, then. If you get stopped, if you're boxed in and it looks like the 'Skyers will get the Crawler, what happens?"

Resigned, Roma fell back on catechism. "Twenty seconds to disconnect and evacuate. Then Central activates the thermite."

"You've got it," Coates grinned. "And I'll be Central. The switch is in my hand. Be slow getting out and . . . ." It was always his final argument.

Roma squirmed in his chair. Deliverymen called it, with the gallows humor they all affected, the hot seat. For Lee it was more than that. It was a vantage point from which to test his preconceptions about Opensky. His whole run, still marked on the console before him but shortening now as he approached 70th Street, became a paradigm of his disagreement with Coates. If he could finish the run safely, his way, it would prove something. Like the child's game: if I don't step on a crack all the way home, I'll get that new bike for my birthday. And now, if Roma could complete the run without any run-in or violence from the 'Skyers, it would prove him right, Coates wrong. The 'Skyers weren't a real menace, only misguided. Only people reacting to the challenge of power, and wealth, and authority, represented by the Crawlers themselves.

He reached 70th Street without incident. His spirits rose. And while the Crawler responded to the automatic gestures of his controlling hand, he began to formulate a plan. What would happen if deliveries were made openly, without all this secrecy and flaunted power? When he got back, he would suggest it.

Daylight was a milky silence outside the Crawler. Here in Workring he saw the lighted factories on each side, smoke belching from chimneys, the streets cleared, wide, and empty. He straddled an invisible line down the center of the street and thundered on toward Renault. Once, passing a factory entrance, he saw the armed watchmen raise gloved hands in greeting, their faces hidden behind the gasmasks necessary in the fetid air. Ash lifted fluttering on the breeze of his passage. Yellow sulfur clouds poured from a pair of stacks to his left.

With a grin, Roma flicked the mike switch. "Crawler ten here."

"Central here. What's the problem?"

"No problem, Central. Position report. On 70th a mile from Renault. All routine. No difficulty."

"You had to say it, right Roma? I've got seven Crawlers out, and you had to interrupt to brag. What do you know about 'routine'? Now get the hell off the horn!"

"Sir." His grin widened. Why not rub it in a little? Coates never missed a chance. Let him take what he dished out.

Through Opensky, into the security of Workring, Roma could now afford to relax. He shut down the heat sensors, unnecessary in full daylight, and relied on the viewers. Humming to himself, he slid into an angled bend in the street. He locked first one tread, then the other, but kept the throttle open. And the Crawler danced around the sharp corner, slamming right-left-right. He slid out of the angle. And into a cul-de-sac.

He locked both treads and skewed to a shuddering stop. This was wrong! The street should have continued on through, but fifty feet ahead of him stood a two-story brick wall. Momentarily bewildered, he reviewed his mental map of 70th Street—a thoroughfare, kept open and unobstructed, or so Coates had taught them.

'Skyers.

The sharp bend in the street, that was it. Roma had somehow swung off 70th and into this dead-end.

He stood on the right tread lock and opened the throttle to spin back the way he'd come. There, lying in the street, was a young girl writhing in pain. Instantly the entire scene etched itself on his mind: a girl in workclothes, looked about 16, right leg twisted underneath her. Left leg . . . gone. Missing! A pink smear on the pavement. And her arms flailing.

Only then did he hear her crying out in pain. He'd done it, run her down with the Crawler roaring blindly into this cul-de-sac. Crippled.

Vomit splashed over his bare thighs and he heard the shaking in his hands as the engine whined to overspeed and died under the surging throttle he twisted unknowingly. He acted instantly. Without thinking he snatched loose the four linkages that tied him to Central, palmed open the hatch, and staggered over the side toward the girl.

Through the roaring in his ears he heard an unintelligible voice from the Crawler cabin, then felt something—someone—hit him behind the knees and hurl him to the cold pavement. Commotion filled the street—silent running bodies bursting on him from all sides, then past him to the Crawler. He rolled onto his side to rise. Through the silent melee he saw the girl lifted erect by two men, handed crutches on which she moved to the corner with practiced grace.

He scrambled to his feet to shout after her but she didn't look back. He took one tentative step and then a soft *thump* whirled him around.

The Crawler cabin spewed white smoke. One man leapt from the smoke with his hair a smoldering mass. He lay screaming in the street while a boy batted at his flaming crown. Still the mob worked silently. The rear cargo hatch popped open. They passed large cartons from hand to hand, snatching them up and tossing them free from the flames that rose to engulf the Crawler.

Roma ran. He ran with the fear of death at his back and a strength of panic he didn't understand, ran from the cul-de-sac, along a cross street, behind a crumbling wall, and out again onto 70th.

Later, he remembered nothing of the distance he had run, only the cold air biting at his bare skin, and the imagined sound of footsteps at his back. The crew at the Renault drop-point, warned by Coates, recognized Roma in his scant trunks. They took him inside where—an hour later—he had calmed enough to talk.

"Kid. Coates is gonna have your ass." The older of the two men at Renault sat facing Lee across a small table. "You know what a Crawler costs?"

"Screw the Crawler. What about them?" The second man sat at a bank of screens and indicated a line of quiet people in the street outside. "Tell him, Klema. How long have they been waiting out there?"

The older man nodded. "Baker's right. We're at the end of the line out here. Only three loads a week for us, and now you cost us this one."

Roma flushed. "Okay. I know that. But I couldn't—"

"And you were gonna be one of the good ones, Coates told us. You know what happens now?" Klema rose to indicate the queue of people outside. They been coming here, some of them, for months. But just once we can't supply 'em, they'll get what they want from the 'Skyers. We lost 'em now. *You* lost 'em.

"It wasn't much," Roma muttered. "Most of the load burned before they could get it out."

"Wonderful!" Baker shook his head. "That's great. And I'll bet you don't even know what the load was."

"Nobody told me."

"Ahh, hell!" Baker turned away in disgust.

Klema looked puzzled. "All you had to do was ask. Didn't that matter to you? What was this—some kind of game? You didn't even ask Coates what you were carrying?"

"What does it matter now?" Lee couldn't look at them.

"Ahh, hell! See what I mean?" Baker spun away from the screen and stalked out of the room. "Keep him away from me, Klema. I don't even want to see him. Soft-headed kid."

The older man shrugged. "Maybe you're right, Roma. Maybe it doesn't matter. Milk. You had a ton of powdered milk. We been out of it for over a week."

"Milk!" It was Lee's turn to be angry. "I risked my life for *milk?*"

"They do." Klema waved at the screen.

"But it could have been something *important*! A run that long, for *milk?*"

After a long moment, Klema said, "There'll be another run in two days. You can go back to City with him."

"Go back? What for? Why should I—"

"Because you're not worth a damn out here. And if I was you, I wouldn't talk to Baker till then. People who mess up aren't his best friends, you know. Even smart people and volunteers."

"What about you?" Roma's question sounded like a plea. "You're in charge here. What do you think?"

Klema shrugged. "I just do a job, kid. Counseling's out of my line." He went after Baker.

Roma stared at the screen, and at the line of people waiting outside.

Heel!

first published in *Amazing Science Fiction Stories*, November 1975

Click, click, click.

Carl Boyce sat huddled in the recessed doorway of an abandoned sporting goods shop. Two signs, one torn and peeling loose from the glass, showed through the grimy window to his left: "Hunting and Fishing Licenses," and a hand-lettered "Available—Newton Realty."

Click, click, click.

The sound of each marching stiletto heel striking the pavement drove shivers through him. He cursed his own carelessness. The pale gray dawn had caught him unescorted, several blocks from the nearest Shelter. And then it had been too late to run. They would have seen him at once, converged on him with the instinct they had all developed so quickly. Another man might have tried; Carl Boyce didn't dare.

If he tried to brazen it out now and walked calmly through the nearly deserted streets, there would be questions. He couldn't face the questions again.

Nor could he hold out much longer where he lay. He had not eaten since yesterday noon. A tic plucked at his left eyelid and his stomach growled discomfort, a burning acid rumble that gnawed at him. He doubled over, pressed both knotted fists into his gut, and tried to think rationally. He felt dizzy with hunger, light-headed. He had to plan something soon. Even now he was not certain he could outrun them.

He risked another glance outside. There were more of them now. Eight women, "cruising"—their word for it. Across the street one of them paced the sidewalk and smiled vacantly into each store window as she passed, hoping that someone inside might respond. She couldn't have been more than sixteen but already wore the look of a predator. Her eyes glittered cold, and the taut cords of her neck belied the carefully rehearsed, soft smile she wore.

Not her, he decided. The young ones were too demanding. Better to wait for one of the more matronly sorts who strolled the city's empty canyons. Like that one a month ago who had wanted nothing but conversation. They all said that, but she had actually meant it. He had spent four days with her, until a neighbor became too inquisitive. Then he had run again.

Nearly seven months of running.

He searched the street for inspiration. And found it! His problem solved itself. A woman standing across the street was staring his way. She had seen him. He had nothing to do but wait.

She walked slowly toward him. He recognized the caution that slowed her stride. If she hurried, the others might understand.

Or perhaps she delayed for his sake. It was a nice touch, not to rush him. She walked like someone approaching a wary colt. It gave him the chance to size her up. Long auburn hair framed a maturing face, neither young nor old. She looked to be in her thirties, though Carl had never been good a guessing their ages. On her, the transparent coat they all wore spoke modesty; beneath it she wore pasties and bikini briefs. She was too heavy for his taste—a bitter laugh bubbled in his throat; as if his taste mattered any more. And the high heels on which she clicked toward him did little to disguise her thick ankles. With each step, the dimpled flesh of her thighs trembled.

She stopped on the sidewalk in front of his hiding place and stared away down the street as if searching for something. Without looking his way she asked, "Waiting for a friend?" Her low voice carried well.

He rose to his feet awkwardly.

"One minute," she whispered. She turned away and elaborately lit a cigarette. Her position screened him from two younger ones who clicked past. Then she backed into the doorway.

Still she didn't look directly at him. "I was just going to lunch. Join me?"

He crooked his elbow and let her grasp his bicep with one hand. They all enjoyed it that way.

"Call me Beth," she said.

He nodded, and they walked out into the sunlight.

His presence changed the street. The marching heels fell silent as women up and down the block caught sight of him. Some shrugged commiseration with one another. A few studied Beth with frankly puzzled appraisals. The young one he had noticed moments before crossed the street and posed in the center of the sidewalk ahead of them, blocking their path. She ran a thick tongue over parted teeth and ground her upthrust hips around an imaginary point in mid-air between them.

"I know some fun threesies," she rasped.

Beth tightened her grip on his arm and urged him past the girl.

Raucous laughter followed them into the restaurant.

A designer's idea of masculinity dominated the place oppressively. It was dark and paneled, leather-lined and massive. In the cool darkness Carl felt weak again, as if their passage through the stares outside had sapped what little strength remained to him. Beth guided him possessively past the queue of waiting singles toward the maitre d'.

With a smirk and raised eyebrows for greeting, he guided them officiously to a table where he pulled out a chair. The seat touched Carl behind the knees; he collapsed gratefully into it. The maitre d' reached past to lay menus on the table and gently brushed a hand across the back of Carl's neck.

"Keep your goddamn paws to yourself!"

The silent women staring from all sides broke into smiles or nodded at one another with patronizing titters. Beth preened in the glow of attention she felt directed her way.

She waited till the maitre d' had sulked out of earshot. "You see more and more of them lately, don't you think, Mr. . . . ?"

"Charley. My name's Charley." He watched the maitre d' mince toward the foyer and wondered why he couldn't learn to imitate that gait. He had tried. God knows he had tried. For weeks, that time in Pittsburgh, he had affect a lisp, worn mascara and velvet, but nothing seemed to work for him. He couldn't fool the stalkers for long. He knew they were out there, somewhere, hunting him.

". . . have, Charles?"

"What? Oh—uh, you order. It's up to you." Half-eaten meals decorating the tables all around him filled his mouth with saliva.

She ordered, then motioned the wine stewardess over and whispered to her.

Carl scrubbed his scarred knuckles and pulled his collar loose. He wished they wouldn't stare so blatantly. He was certain some of them could recognize him. He had shaved off his moustache as soon as the posters began to appear, and he had seen none of the posters since arriving in Chicago. But the stares still frightened him. The stalkers studied the wanted lists carefully, and they want *him*. Not any man. Carl Boyce.

Beth tried to engage him in conversation, talking about sports, feigning an interest he saw through at once, shifting rapidly from one "male" subject to another. He did little but nod in response. He had never been able to share in the banter and small talk that women seemed to expect of him, not even before . . . he blocked the thought.

While he waited for the meal to arrive one thumb idly traced the grain in the table edge. The old feeling came through his hands to surprise him—the table was real wood, not plastic, not some cheap composition board. He leaned back in his chair to glance down and saw the long sweeping curl of split oak. He dug a nail into the grain but caught himself doing so and jerked back. No good. By now they all knew Carl Boyce had been a cabinet maker, before . . .

For a long moment he held his breath and waited, tensed. No one had noticed.

Beth's broad smile frightened him suddenly, till he realized she was staring over his shoulder. He turned awkwardly to see the wine stewardess carrying a silver tray toward them. On it, a bottle of Michelob.

"Right from the bottle, Charles. That's the way my husband

always drank it. Funny," her eyes grew vacant as she mused over some private memory. "I never—"

"Mine was the same way." A woman at the next table leaned close to interrupt and pat Beth's hand.

Beth froze, and Carl said, "Okay lady. We're talking here. Want to butt out?"

The intruder jerked away as if stung.

"Thank you, Charles, but I understand," Beth said. "I didn't mean to mention my husband, but I *was* married, you know. Many of us were married, before..."

The disease first appeared in Iran, though no one considered it serious at the time. Neither did anyone suspect that something so simple as an unexplained outbreak of mumps among the frontline troops might have been "caused." The number of cases multiplied rapidly, unchecked, all but unnoticed in the medical reports, freighted down as they were with lists of the war-dead and seriously wounded. A Navy doctor in Tel Aviv doubted the first reports he noticed; he simply knew better than to accept as fact the unlikely statistics that crossed his desk. Virtually all American adults have already had mumps—simple parotitis—along with other relatively harmless childhood diseases; have had them, or been inoculated against them. Thus when the doctor read that 40% of our combat troops in Iran had contracted a particularly virulent strain of the disease, he did what seemed to him logical: he put the decimal point where he thought it belonged and forwarded the reports to Washington.

No one in Washington could be expected to concern himself with the lucky 4% sent to the rear to recover from mumps in row upon growing row of hospital tents.

The medics felt put upon by the added burden of malingerers who faked both lethargy and severe headaches; they were already swamped with combat casualties. When those same malingerers died in masses, it was too late. The medics recorded the deaths on the proper forms and sent the bodies home.

In Cairo a curious doctor named Robert Shallot performed several unauthorized autopsies on corpses ostensibly in transit. He flew to Washington to report on his discovery of a disease he termed "Shallot's parotitis encephalitis." That small bid for immortality did little for him; within a month he died of "his" disease. The entire male staff of Walter Reed Hospital followed him a week later.

No one ever learned what the disease had been termed by the Chinese virologist whose submicroscopic miracle had altered the structure of a simple virus. Perhaps it bore his name. It didn't matter. The inoculations which had protected most Chinese troops—all but the few infected volunteers who surrendered to the Americans to spread the disease—soon proved ineffectual. The virus continued mutating. The learned doctor's greatest success lay in the ease with which the virus spread not only through human contact but also from one arthropod vector to another. Within two months nearly every spider, crustacean, and millipede on the face of the globe was a carrier.

Whether or not the doctor intended his creation to behave as it did, women were less affected than men. Only twenty percent of American women died, no more than twenty-two million. Men fared less well. They died in numbers so nearly approaching one hundred percent that only a carping statistician would quibble, at the third decimal point.

Too late, a reasonably effective antigen was developed by a pair of British virologists. Ganders and Price were their names. They were roommates and for weeks had merely discussed the headlines which forecast the end of the species as country after country saw its male population eliminated: mumps, followed by orchitis, followed by encephalitis, followed by death. As women, Ganders and Price were of the lucky eighty percent and immune; as lesbians, they considered but felt little emotion at the thought of a manless world; as scientists, they attacked the merely intellectual puzzle involved in conquering a disease that promised to affect their own relationship in no important way.

In other days, they might have won the Nobel Prize. The Nobel Committee had disbanded with the death of all but two of its members. Two women.

Throughout the world chaos spread the truth of what Women's Liberation groups in American had long claimed: men ran everything. With men dead or dying, every major enterprise ground to a halt. The war in the Middle East was over.

President-by-default Betty Friedan signed a peace treaty with the fifth Madame Mao, renegotiated non-aggression pacts with women representatives of all the major powers, and civilization started over.

But some men proved naturally immune. Not many, and there appeared no common factor to designate them. But here and there a man survived. Because of the breakdown in communications that accompanied the chaos, no one was certain how many. The few female statisticians at work couldn't collect adequate data, but the number of surviving males was infinitesimal by any standards.

The Ganders-Price serum halted the spread of the disease though it effected no cures.

What few men survived were sterile.

"After Harry died, I didn't know what would happen to me," Beth said. "We'd only been married a few months. It just wasn't fair. Why him? I kept asking myself. Why him, and not all the others too?" She blushed suddenly and waved a helpless hand at Carl.

He nodded. Sooner or later they all said the same thing. He had no answer. No one had an answer. Some lived, some died. No sense looking for reasons. He bent low over his plate and shoved chunks of steak into his mouth. Out of the corner of his eye he could seem them watching him but he was too hungry to care. Besides, they liked it that way—a man should be coarse, hungry. It was part of the mystique.

"I'm sorry, Charles. It's just that . . . well. I hated you all, and that's the truth."

"Sure it is," he mumbled. "For couple months, maybe, you hated us."

She blushed again, and he remembered.

At first the neighbors avoided him. But his wife Irma knew what would eventually happen. She enjoyed those early days. She had status, her own man, her own household. They were the good days. Then the neighbors' hatred waned, replaced by tentative and uncertain attitudes that only Irma had expected. First there was Mrs. Kohl, their next-door neighbor, bringing over an occasional suet pudding. "I know you don't make it, Irma," she said. "And I've got nobody to do for anymore. What's it hurt? I just like to see a man eat."

It didn't stop there. Soon the invitations weren't casual or cryptic any longer. "Carl, come help me turn the mattress. I need a man." "Carl? Irma treating you all right? She's just a kid, don't know what a man really likes." Or, "I filled the pool today, Carl. You ever do it underwater? I'll show you a good time."

He and Irma quarreled about it at first. But to hold onto him she agreed to a compromise: four nights a week he stayed home; three nights a week he visited his neighbors. That seemed to work out. Irma took pride in his reputation and began to expect favors from the neighborhood women who didn't want their names noted on the blacklist she made Carl respect. Once or twice she objected to neighbors inviting friends in on the nights Carl visited them, but not too strenuously. The census showed 287 surviving men in Philadelphia, few of them with Carl's following. It made Irma proud.

Carl's pride waned slowly. Whenever he tried to talk to them they pretended interest, but not very well. He loved hockey; he never found a woman who had the slightest understanding of the game. He was a cabinet maker, an artist of sorts. He offered to build a china cupboard for that one named Irene-something who had her bedroom lined with mirrors. She agreed, then couldn't keep her hands off him while he worked. They were all the same, one thing on their minds. None of them respected him as a person, not even Irma. He had become her prize possession, more important to her than the pink Thunderbird he earned from a Ford dealer's widow. It all began to disgust him.

". . . Disgusting, at first, if you don't mind my saying so. But times change, I guess. If men can stand the way they're treated, it's nothing to me. Would you like another beer?"

Carl shook his head. "No thanks." He leaned back to loosen his belt. Because they were all watching, he belched loudly. "That was good." He watched the maitre d' hovering beside a table nearby where three women had long since finished but sat dawdling over coffee. It was clear they wouldn't leave until Carl did.

"What kind of work did you do, before . . . ?"

"Doesn't matter, does it?" He saw the hurt blossom in her eyes. "Okay, I'm sorry. I sold insurance." The lie came easily. The truth might have identified him. Even here in Chicago telecasts would have given his biography. Beth might have heard them, might have seen the posters. For a week after leaving Pittsburgh on his escape west he had carried one of the posters, folded in his wallet, in a way proud of the reward offered. That Mexican boy—the one they caught in Dallas—had been posted at $50,000. The reward for Carl Boyce was nearly a quarter of a million dollars. And he was worth it.

He had often wondered how the Mexico kid had accepted his capture. He'd been on the run, as Carl was. Since being caught, he had disappeared. No word at all. The Dallas Population Board had hidden him away.

"Sure I'm sure. Martinez was his name. I seen him once on the TV, when they started playing him up so big like they did. Kid must have been nuts to run. He had everything he wanted."

Carl sat in the lounge of the Philadelphia Men's Shelter and stared at the ceiling, hands clasped behind his head. He listened to the argument but stayed out of it. He couldn't afford to draw attention to himself, even here, in the comparative safety of the Shelter. The Stalkers had spies everywhere. Anyone might turn him in, if they learned the truth about him. He had just discovered it himself.

"This Martinez kid stood here next to a whole row of cribs. Twenty-some kids that little greaser had the first year. They treated him like he was a little tin god. Can you feature a white woman letting him get in her knickers? But some of them done it."

"You're bitching 'cause you keep firing blanks like the rest of us."

"So what? Don't I get everything I need? Not all of them wants kids."

"We could have had children, did I say that?" Beth looked at him with pain evident in her expressive eyes. "We were only waiting till Harry got another raise."

"Must have been tough," Carl muttered. Still the stares surrounded him. Tension returned to settle in his left eyelid, it tugged at his concentration and twitched like a metronome. He might have to leave with Beth, if only to keep the others from following him and waiting outside the Shelter. It was risky being seen entering any Shelter; they immediately began parading before the closed-circuit TV cameras that sent video to every room. Carl had once enjoyed sitting in the comfort of a private room, or in the common lounge, examining the silent lineup of eager women waiting for him to make a choice among them. And with no audio in the system, he couldn't hear the constant clatter of their heels. Now that pleasure was behind him. Even the Shelter was no longer a haven; they knew about Carl Boyce.

He shuddered at the memory. The day he discovered . . .

"Carl! What do you think?" Irma tapped his shoulder and woke him. He had fallen asleep watching another re-run of the 2015 Super Bowl. Packers again. Each afternoon, when women were off at work, the networks ran shows intended to entertain the few men in the audience. Carl had seen all the reruns several times, but nothing else on TV interested him—certainly not the soap operas that filled prime time, with women playing men's parts, acting out fantasies he had grown sick of hearing whispered in his ear by every lonely woman he favored with his attention.

"What do I think about what?"

"Lana Kohl. She's pregnant!"

"Bullshit. She's faking it. You know her imagination. Or maybe it's only whadayacallit, 'psychosomatic.'"

"No. I mean it. She's seen three specialists. There's no doubt."

"Okay then, who's the hero?"

"That's what I'm saying. It's *you*! She swears it. There wasn't anybody else it could have been."

"Yeah, sure." He waved her away and turned back to the TV screen. Less than thirty seconds left in the game. Time for the winning field goal. Damn Packers! If he concentrated hard enough he could almost pretend it might be blocked this time.

In two days he knew. Irma had been right. There were three pregnancies on his block, another in Germantown. The woman there claimed he had done it at one of Lana Kohl's parties.

He was an instant celebrity. Of the 287 adult males in Philadelphia, only one other had caused conception, and Carl hadn't heard a word about him in nearly three months. Some doctors had begun to hope for spontaneous remission of the sterility in all men, though none believed very seriously in that possibility. A few men had survived the plague; fewer yet could father children. Carl was one of those few.

Somehow women learned his unlisted phone number. Changing it did no good. Within hours, they had the new number. He tore out the phone.

Lines formed outside his house.

Irma tried to delude herself for a few tense days but finally had to accept a new definition: *she* was barren; *she* couldn't conceive. In the midst of her anguish she slashed her wrists and quietly bled to death in the bathtub while Carl was busy on the couch with one of the applicants who had caught his fancy.

To protect him from the swelling mobs, the Philadelphia Population Board drugged him and took him to a hospital in the Poconos. When he regained consciousness, the Government psychiatrists began to "redefine his role."

"Do you have the time?" Beth asked.

"Sure. It's—"

"Almost two," the woman at the next table interrupted. "If you have to go somewhere, I can drop your friend at the Shelter."

"I'm not staying at the Shelter, lady. Beth and me are going home now. Is that okay with you?'

Beth turned wide eyes to him. "Really? I was *hoping* you . . . Never mind. Let me pay the check."

He watched her scatter bills on the table and stumble to her feet. Through the room sighs crested to a droning murmur. He walked to the door, eyes straight ahead. The code would protect him, till they escaped this mob. None of the others would grow too aggressive so long as he stayed with Beth.

She clutched his arm at the door and looked a silent question at him.

He felt sympathy for her. "Why not?" he answered. "I was married, too, before . . . Only my wife, she kil . . . She's dead." Her hand tightened on his arm. "It's okay now. I was just thinking. It must of hit you hard, to lose your man. Some of them don't know about that." He waved a thumb back toward the scores of heads turned his way. "We should all try and understand each other."

"Understanding, Mr. Boyce," the psychiatrist said. She bridged her fingertips and looked at Carl with a self-assurance that irritated him. "Try to understand the way a woman feels when her biological nature is denied. Life is meant to beget life."

"I'm not arguing, am I? I'm just saying, sex isn't the only thing there is. A man has his work to do. You ever see a piece of cherrywood that's been oiled and hand-rubbed till it looks like glass? Well, that's what I'm talking about. But you, all you want me for is to breed, like some goddamn stud horse. I'll do my share, but I've got a life to live, too."

"No one plans to deprive you of anything, Mr. Boyce. We quite understand. We're only suggesting that science offers more efficient ways than nature. You could scarcely be expected to—uh—'service' more than a dozen or so women a week, and with such frequent activity, there'd be little chance for viable spermatozoa to develop. It's not that we expect *more* of you. Rather, I'd say, less. But through artificial means we could multiply the positive effects a hundred-fold. And with no ill effects to you. How can you object?"

"I'm not objecting. Just let me make up my own mind. Stop pushing."

"You have to think beyond yourself." She raised her voice as if lecturing to a large class. "Mankind is more important than any individual."

"Uh-huh. The last time somebody tried giving me that line it was a Top Sergeant in the desert. I was a dumb kid he wanted to stick out on point on a night patrol. Well, I'm telling you what I told him. That's all well and good, except *I'm* the individual you keep talking about."

For nearly five days he floundered through weaker and weaker rationalizations. Then he gave in.

They isolated him for forty-eight hours.

They took him to a lab. It was cool. It was antiseptic. The walls were all white. Everything was impersonal. No one called him by name. Two doctors were there. Three others entered to observe. He was nearly unable to cooperate. They induced ejaculation mechanically. They dismissed him.

Their unsmiling thanks made him feel dirty; stained.

The orderly conducting him back to his room down the long empty corridors propositioned him. He let himself be led into a linen closet. He removed her smock and eased her back onto a pile of blankets. Then he kicked her twice in the groin and left her pale and gasping where she lay.

He drove the stolen ambulance nearly a mile before he was sick. For two days the stench of vomit burned his nostrils, but by then he was seventy miles away and running hard.

He sat in the car beside Beth and shook his head at the cautious way she threaded her way through the slight mid-town traffic toward the Outer Drive.

"When did you say you left the East Coast?"

"I never said I did."

"Sorry. It's your accent. Sort of eastern."

"Look. Maybe you ought to let me out here."

She bowed her head over the wheel. "I was just making conversation."

They drove in silence.

She stopped before one of the highrise condominiums towering beside Lake Michigan and handed the car keys to the doorgirl. She clicked across the sidewalk and Carl followed her inside.

Her apartment was rich-looking without the fussiness Carl expected. He shuffled through the deep-pile carpet and stood looking out through sliding glass doors across the balcony toward the lake. He waited for her to "change."

She surprised him by reappearing in a long cotton housecoat and carrying a drink in each hand.

"Let's talk, all right?"

He took the glass and sat next to her on the couch.

She talked. After a few confused moments he understood what she was saying. "I've heard about it. Artificial insemination—just using those poor men. No one ever stops to think how they must feel, to be treated like breeding stock. And the rewards they post! I couldn't face myself in the mirror if I took that kind of money. I'd feel like a bounty hunter."

Before he could catch himself he had launched into the tirade he had muttered to himself so many times during the past lonesome, running months. He heard little of what he said, his fear and anger and bewilderment spewed out in gobbets of strangled curses and complaints and left him drained.

Then she was holding his hand, and they were both quiet.

"I knew that, Carl. Of course you feel that way. But please don't let it make you bitter. Think of their point of view. Not only the women who want children, though there are enough of those I guess, but all the others too, the ones who can't let themselves consider the feelings of one man when the race is threatened. They've got their minds bent on rebuilding a world. Ambition does terrible things to people."

"How did you know my name?"

She smiled wryly. "Slipped out, didn't it? But after thinking of you as Carl all these months, it had to happen."

"How long have you been after me?"

"Quite a while. But it's not what you think."

His back-handed slap caught her high on the cheek. "Don't snow me, lady. That's been tried by experts." He lunged to his feet and started toward the door.

"Carl? Wait. Look there, to your left."

He followed her pointing finger to an old fashioned chiffonier visible through the bedroom doorway. And recognized it. Cross-grained maple rubbed to a silky luster, brass fittings on the drawers. His. An early piece, lovingly crafted over a winter of evenings in his own basement workshop. He knew it as he knew himself: all mortise and tenon joints, not a screw or nail in it—a creation, not a construct.

He turned a puzzled look toward her.

"I bought it from a woman in Philadelphia over a year ago. It wasn't till later that I read about you in the papers. Now, if you don't believe that, you can leave."

"What's your point? Am I supposed to fall down in a faint from gratitude?"

She touched her sore cheek gingerly. "No, you're not the type. I only hope you might believe me when I say I was trying to find the man who made that. I thought he might be special. Someone I might like to know."

He let the silence stretch between them. When her expression didn't change, he smiled. Then he laughed. Then ran to swing her off her feet in a wide circle, roaring his delight with her, and with himself, and with the sheltered corner of the world he'd found.

He enjoyed the slight resistance she feigned when he slipped the robe from her shoulders and forced her down to the couch.

They lay together on the floor, sated. Darkness outside had converted the glass balcony doors to a mirror in which he saw the chandelier flickering its mute yellow tongues. He was surprised to see the couch above them and couldn't remember having left it. "Good," he said. "Not like with the others."

"Frame of mind. That's the whole difference, they say." She ran a fingernail down his bare chest.

His foolish grin faded when a knock sounded at the door. "Who is it?" he whispered.

She stood and smiled at him. "I guess time's up, that's all."

He leaped toward the balcony door but saw two of them, in stiletto heels, standing outside, waiting in the darkness.

"They changed the reward," she said softly. "The money and the full day with you."

"But you said—"

"Believe me, it wasn't the money. Please believe that."

The apartment door opened. Two of them entered. One asked, "Where'd you find him?"

"Sporting goods store—part of the pattern," Beth answered. "A 'masculine' hiding place, just as we thought."

"Was it the bureau? What pinned him down?"

Beth shrugged. "They all give in. Just a matter of the right woman, the right time and place."

Carl searched his mind for an angry response but found only resignation.

When they converged on him their heels made no sound on the thick carpet.

Fragments of a Second Friday

first published in *TRACKS*, Fall 1976

Second Friday.

Criminologists, politicians, and *The Times* call it Memory Day.

The underground press calls it High Time (source—an editorial in the *National Observer*, reading: "To preclude recidivism, it is high time we heed the appeals of victims of these heinous...")

The people call it Second Friday. Outside any State Restitution-Recall Center, on Second Friday, count the crowd. Check ages. Look for outré costumes, or the knowledgeable glint in certain eyes. See the faces. Tics there, some of them. Some lazy-lidded casual. All waiting. Know the crowd, you can know the crime being "prevented"... inside the R-R Center.

This crowd, this Second Friday, offers definition: twenty-seven girls stamping in the frosty air. Their breaths hang steam puffs in the morning sun. Parked across the street, a cameraman shoots footage for some sun-bronzed mannequin to mumble pieties over on the six peem news.

One man, a fragile fifty, walks trembling at his unaccustomed courage and pantomimes a work-bound passerby. He has passed by four times in the last hour.

And the girls: blue-kneed in micro-minis, gooseflesh, henna, velveteen. Average age, fourteen. They might be a scout troop after merit badges. They wait, salivate—everyone has a role in street theater. Call it an encounter group.

Allie Pench shuffled down the white-tiled corridor. They had taken his shoes, pants, shirt, everything. They had shaved his shadowed jowls as if that careful scraping might remove coarseness more ingrained than surface. The smock he wore was white paper, a stiff and crackling tent that didn't fit but accompanied him as he walked, hanging open down the back. He walked in a parody of parade rest, his grasping fists behind him holding tight a crinkled seam, his elbows hanging sharp angles like featherless wings. He shuffled to retain white paper slippers over veined, sclerotic feet. Dressed in white, shod in white, led down a white tunnel where his slippers whispered echoes in the antiseptic air—Allie Pench.

"A goddamned waste of time," he said.

The woman leading the way, Dr. Delores Cain, ignored him.

He knew the type. Education up to here, toothy smiles and soft-spoken, but crotch like a carp's gill, all split shake shingle razor blade and sandpaper. Few minutes alone with her, he'd bring her down. Have her begging. One thing for her kind, couple pounds Allie Pench's meat injections, that'd do her right.

"Hey! You listening to me?"

"This way, Mr. Pench. We're almost there."

Mister Pench, Mister Pench. Nobody'd called him anything but Allie, ever. And she knew it, this one. Snooty righteousness, too good for him, her and the others. Even the judge—oh so sad in pronouncing sentence, only doing his duty. Soft word turneth away wrath. That stuff. Well, let them try. It wasn't working with Allie.

"Hey lady! How's your wrath?" His snigger was a nervous whinny.

". . . no longer even vaguely experimental. I hope I've made that perfectly clear." Claude Onderdonk stared up at the faces filling the small amphitheatre as if to dare a question. "I'm frankly surprised so many of you felt it necessary to observe today. I'd have thought, after three years, the novelty would have worn off. If you're looking for something sensational, you're wasting your time. The trash you've been reading—yes, and writing, some of you—is more sensational than anything you'll see here. A few—"

"Tell it to the crowd out front, Warden." One voice from the tier of reporters.

Onderdonk peered into the shadows. "Who got them here? It wasn't the Kramer girl, I'll promise you that. As far as she's concerned the whole episode never happened. It's only the newspapers that keep crying for vengeance. Well, vengeance isn't our business. Prevention is, and that's—"

"Nice prevention, after the fact."

Onderdonk motioned, and a white-coated guard helped the reporter from the room, one hand clamped on the neck with a still forefinger tucked high behind the reporter's ear.

"All right. In case there's someone here for the first time, I'll go through the history again. The medicos can explain it better than I, and you can pick up one of the printed handouts as you leave. All the names and dates are there, general background as well as specific procedures in this case."

Warden Onderdonk spun the rheostat beside the glass panel centered in the front wall. The lights in the amphitheatre dimmed. "He'll be in there, behind the glass. The Kramer girl too, just as a check. Watch for yourself."

The tunnel ended at a gray door. Allie followed his guide—nurse? guard?—through the narrow doorway with practiced swagger. They weren't getting to Allie Pench. Inside the operating room, two people waited: a tall doctor beside a chair, Lois Kramer seated in another.

"What the hell is this?" Allie grabbed the woman's wrist and jerked her around to face him. He spoke in a hoarse whisper. "What's she doing here?"

With thumb and forefinger, Delores Cain lifted and dropped his hand.

The doctor spoke. "Lois? This is Mister Pench."

"We want you to talk to him," Dr. Cain said. She nodded. The tall male doctor pressed a tube against Lois's neck. A hiss. The smell of sugar.

Lois smiled. One hand waved, then brushed at her neck as if to shoo mosquitoes. "Sure. What should we talk about?" She laid bare hands on her bare knees.

Allie looked away. Goddamned paper robe rustled and revealed his trembling. The room—white again, white—began dissolving. Hard to breathe now and images piled uninvited in behind his eyes, recalled, vivid: snowflakes falling to a melting street; car, warm inside and fetid, on the floor in back, gum wrappers and torn silk, ghost-white thighs—white—against a patterned fabric. Then, *lights!* Noses pressed against the windows, misted inside, then *shouts!* And motion. Action. Jostling movements. Allie, cold, bare-legged in the street.

"Not many recall their first memory tap. It's one of those paradoxes. We all seem to repress any recollection of the first procedure, a common side-effect, normal I guess for ten-year-olds. But everyone remembers the tap the medicos take at age twenty. Briefly, here's a summary of procedures, in uh . . . in layman's language." Onderdonk looked up from the paper in his hand. He knew all eyes focused through the one-way glass and on the scene playing out behind him but he carried on with ritual. Second Friday.

"A short-focal laser inserted up the left nostril. Slight tissue burn to widen a dendrite canal into the forebrain. Insertion of a curette. Cuttings taken. Then centrifuge, distillation, a culture-medium to grow a quantity of the base. Once the base is fixed, it's sealed and stored in the R-R vaults. First tap, age ten. Oh!" He glanced up again. "That's why we didn't like tapping the Kramer girl so soon. She's only thirteen and . . ."

They ignored him.

"All right. At age twenty, injections of magnesium pemoline to stimulate RNA production in the forebrain, then a second tap. To date our records indicate that the base solution, taken in youth, can provide point-nine effectiveness in reversing incipient senility, when we re-inject the aged. It essentially gives them back their youth.

"Then, three years ago, when Clauster and Files discovered the potential for memory transfer—"

"Why's the poor kid in there with Pench? Isn't that rough on her?"

Every month the same questions. Onderdonk closed his eyes to recite. "We tapped immediately for episode sensation retention, then put her through puromycin erasure therapy.

She doesn't remember that day, none of what Pench did, She doesn't remember him at all."

Inside the chamber, Delores Cain said, "You can go now, Lois. Thank you dear"

Lois slid from her chair. "Is Mister Pench sick?"

"Never mind," the other doctor said. "He'll be fine in a few minutes." He showed her out a door centered beneath a large mirror high up in the canted ceiling of the operating room.

Allie found his hands. They hung beside him at the end of rigid arms, and his paper gown gaped open. He snatched at the back, seamed it, protected himself.

"Sit in the chair, Mister Pench."

He looked around. Nothing to stop him from running. Only thing . . . they'd find him again. He'd made his choice: no hard time, only this medical thing. They'd promised him no pain, but his nose still burned. What the hell did they know about pain? Crowds of strangers beating at you, that was pain. And the women! They were the worst. Rotten vindictive bitches.

"Really, Mister Pench. It'll only be a moment." He led Allie to the chair where Delores Cain stood.

"Does she have to be here?"

"Yes, Mister Pench. I have to be here." Her smile was feral.

They did want vengeance, Allie knew. Talk all they wanted about healing instead of punishment. He could smell it on her—musk and sweat. The doctor guy too, a curl to his lips and hands that played with a little silver tube. They were wrong if they thought they could scare Allie Pench.

Fragments of a Second Friday

The sun-bronzed mannequin arrives outside the R-R Center, talks briefly to the cameraman, who grumbles but drags his equipment from the truck.

"Don't blame me, Charlie. They want some interviews with this one." The mannequin approaches a pair of girls standing aside from the milling crown. "Girls? Look this way?"

He turns. "Got a level, Charlie?"

The cameraman nods and hoists a frame over his head, letting it rest on his shoulders. He shrugs to settle the weight of the handicam, snaps his fingers in front of the mike and watches the needle on the dial dance, then waves. "Gotcha."

"Okay girls. Now . . . we're taping this. Right here. I want to ask you a few questions. Just be natural."

They titter and preen. One whispers to the other and they laugh aloud.

"First, can you tell me why you're here today?"

"It's like, you know, like everybody comes down here, Second Friday." She giggles. To her friend: "Ain't so?"

"Sure, Everybody."

The old man passes by again, watching them unnoticed. He walks on eggs. Scanning left and right. No one pays attention. His path curves slightly till he sidles near the pair engrossed in chatter with the microphone. He's near enough to reach and touch them if he dared. He doesn't. but the possibility so moves him that he darts into a doorway and stands watching, ferret-eyed, his hands deep in his pockets clasped and worshipping.

"What do you expect to see?"

"Well, you know. *Him*."

"He won't be the same when they let him out."

The girls shriek with laughter and fall into each other's arms, yet even in abandon careful not to turn away from Charlie's blinking camera.

The interview continues, ebb and flow as mannequin and girls keep looking for the lens in a shifting myturn, yourturn ego-dance.

"Relax Mister Pench. Only a few minutes more. The doctor took a second silver tube from a wall-hung rack and checked the label. He held it up and asked, "Recognize these, Mister Pench?"

"Yeah." Allie sits and sulks. Okay, they had him, but no law says he's got to like it. Knew a guy once, went through R-R, a torch. Weird guys, used to hold a burning match till it burned down and his fingers blistered, wet his pants, stupid grin on his face the whole time. Torched an abandoned van, a wino flaked out in the thing. Wino got burned bad, the torch got "healed" through R-R on Second Friday. Weird guy, blinks all the time, doesn't like bright lights. But that's nothing to Allie. He doesn't like lights either, big deal.

". . . listen to me Mister Pench. If you ignore us, you'll have to repeat the treatment. Dr. Cain held out one of the vials, her painted nails glistening, and asked, "Can you tell us what this is, Mister Pench?"

"Probably mine, from wherever you keep the stuff."

"Your . . . what?"

"They say it's your memory, only I still got mine." Allie smirked, one up on them. "But this is still sore." He rubbed his nose. "I thought they never tapped nobody after he passed something like twenty, ain't that so?—Hey!" He glanced over his shoulder at the real doctor. "He ain't tapping me again, is he?"

"And this other tube is Lois Kramer's, Mister Pench." She smiled again. "They may look the same, but they're not."

"All right Delores," said the doctor. "Let's get on with it." His face was red as if his collar had suddenly grown too tight. He took both tubes and poured their contents into a single beaker, spun it quickly, then poured the blend back into one tube and capped it.

"No more damn speeches," Allie said. "Do it!"

"Don't you care how it works?" Dr. Cain purred. "You really should, you know."

". . . not exactly certain," Onderdonk said. "There are several theories, but they all boil down to the same thing. We simply don't know. Given the billions of combinations possible to the four RNA codons, multiplied scores of times in a long-chain molecule, there are limitless groupings and sequences. Assume that a certain RNA molecule carries the smell of burning pine, and that once such a molecule is formed it can be transferred to anyone and carry with it that smell. Another may carry the feel of corduroy or the sound of running water. Well, you get the picture.

"For the ennth time, Warden, we get the picture," a reporter in the front row interrupted. "How about some specifics? Can you tell us what they're saying to Pench in there?"

Onderdonk turned to peer through the glass. A peaceful scene, Pench seated and glancing from one doctor to the other. Dr. Cain speaking at the moment, inaudible to those in the observation tiers. He shrugged. "Invasion of privacy for us to listen in. See, uh . . . Washburne vs. State of New

York, sometime two years back. All Doctor Cain's doing now is informing him of his post-treatment rights and obligations. Pench can still refuse Restitution-Recall and accept whatever punishment still obtains under the old statutes. But he won't. None of them do."

"Too damn easy on them."

"One more remark like that and I'll have you taken out. Is that clear?"

Onderdonk stood poised. No answer. His reaching hand found a rheostat and the window went opaque. "Is, that, clear?"

A murmur swept through the amphitheatre. Onderdonk nodded. "See that you remember."

"Tell us about it, Mister Pench. What was it like?

Allie turned to the doctor behind him. "Is that part of the deal? How come I have to say—"

"Tell her!" The doctor looked away. "It's the law."

"That's right, Mister Pench, and we want everything legal and above-board don't we? Remember—you chose R-R. Now if you don't *like* it, there are other—"

"Delores! For God's sake, let the man talk!"

She smiled again. "Objectivity, Doctor." Then a shadow covered her eyes and she lurched forward as if a tension spring had snapped. "Or do you sympathize with this scum?"

Allie said. " All right, let's do it." A few minutes, and done with. "Not much to tell. I seen her on the street. It was snowing. I asked, did she want a ride home, is all. Then we stopped, and . . . and some people come busting in on us. That's it." His voice climbed toward tenor. "I don't know why they said all them things. We was talking, me and her, when this mob

Fragments of a Second Friday

come in and started punchin' me out. You ask me, they're the ones shoulda been arrested, not me. You ever hear of assault and battery?" He twisted awkwardly in his chair. "Mistaken identity, Doc, you ever hear of that? Maybe I only looked like the fella they was after."

"That's the full story, Mister Pench?" Dr. Cain circled his chair, making him squirm and twist to keep her in sight. His paper robe was useless. Damp streaks stained the paper where it clung to his chest, nearly transparent. He tried crossing his legs but the slippers hung loose, and it seemed important for him not to lose what little covering he wore. She stopped and leaned low to whisper, "Lois Kramer had a much better memory of it, I'm sure. Wouldn't you like to find out?"

She jerked her thumb at the man who stepped forward and pressed the silver tube against Allie's neck. A hiss. The smell of ashes.

"Get anything out of that? The mannequin lounging in the back seat watches Charlie reload his camera from the car's glove compartment.

Charlie nods. "We'll cut it, pick out a word here and there. You can dub a voice-over where the kids didn't make any sense." He stared at the milling knot of people for a moment. "Why do you suppose they hang around out here?"

"See themselves on the news, maybe. Who can tell?" The mannequin sneezed, a wet explosion in the cramped car. "I'll be lucky it I don't get laryngitis out of all this. Let's get back."

The old man is no longer in sight. Instead of twenty-seven girls, there are only nine now. A wet drizzle has begun. The nine stand huddled against buildings, trying to use the cover of slight overhangs, but none of them moves to leave. A few check watches. They know it won't be long before *he* comes out. Allie Pench. Having waited this long, they can't give up now. Not without getting what they came for.

He felt stupid. That "Delores" and the guy doc, they had pulled out folding chairs and sat watching him. Neither one blinked. He didn't know what they expected. But damn sure wouldn't give them any satisfaction. He could sit there as long as they could. In a strange way he felt pleased with himself. Whoever said this R-R shit was tough? Beats twenty-five in the slammer, and rape's a sure twenty-five. First time, maybe second, he'd take his chances. But this was number three for old Allie, and that judge was a real bitch. But here Allie was sitting it out. Nothing to it.

Still, the doctors just staring like that, they made him nervous.

"How long you two gonna sit there?" Allie said. His gut churned. The voice wasn't his. Well, it was, but it sounded funny—something different in it, or the way he heard it. "One, two, three, four," he tested. This time he tasted bile in his throat and was afraid to speak again. He closed his eyes against the dizziness that suddenly descended.

"Wait!" burst from him in a frightened squeak. A hand lay on his knee. He peered at the bare leg—nothing there. Really. Nothing! But he could *feel* it, oily wet and sliding up his thigh. That invisible touch so terrified him that he closed his eyes again. Not seeing, he could pretend that it *was* real. And it was, had to be, felt real, plucking at him now, at shorts he didn't wear; and then he lurched forward as his pants were snatched and torn away. Another hand had found his lips and crushed them hard against his teeth till warm blood tasted bitter and the stench of nicotine from chapped and crusted knuckles filled his nostrils. He opened his eyes but saw only the torn headliner of a car, and, as he sought denial of the very facts assaulting him, the hands kept pawing, stroking plucking, pushing here and there, his breasts a swarm of fiery bruises while inside a diamond dot of cold grew tangible and swelled until he thought he's burst with fire outside frost beneath his heart in blistered shards of ice. His breath came harder, not enough to scream, and how he wanted that—to shout, release, break free from all the hands that pressed him down. A coarseness scraped his thighs, his stomach, every bare spot of him—tongue, it was, unshaven jowls, the fetid breath of some dark beast, a dog or other animal unseen but felt at every pore and crevice of him.

Then there was pause. Not peace, but time enough to know the hammer of his heart and feel his surging chest. The hands were there, gone, there, and time was for an instant frozen. He hung in terror on a cliff edge, unable to step back and blinded by the pit beneath him while he tottered. Hung there. Balanced now upon a wire taut but slacking as he hesitated in uncertainty.

Then the fire. Lava seared his groin and drove imprisoned screams through him. Fork tines scored in patterns down his ribs. Vomit choked him as an alien pressure filled him and made him bloat with pain.

There were voices—shouts, cold breezes that defined his sweating, and his tangled hair lay red across his eyes to blur the sight of rushing movement, jerking, a staggered lunge. There were snowflakes and people in the snow. He was crying. They comforted him without comprehension—he was free, and in the joy of that he cried.

Murmurs through the amphitheatre: "See him fall off the chair?" "Good Christ, man! He looked like he had a fit." "How'd you like to watch that once a month?" "And look at that one, the woman in there—crying too. A minute ago she looked ready to gut him."

Onderdonk spun the rheostat and the amphitheatre brightened. He looked at his watch. "In half an hour, we'll have the next one. It's a simple assault case, first conviction. You can stay and watch, if you want to."

Several of the observers rose shakily to their feet and left, with the ironic blessing of Onderdonk's smiles following them out. Most stayed. They scribbled perfunctory notes or leaned back to catch a nap before the next one came in.

Second Friday. 11:30 A.M. Allie Pench shuffles out the side door of the State Restitution-Recall Center, a free man. He walks splay-footed, spraddle-legged tender. He has had a shower and a final lecture, without feeling the hot water or hearing the words. They promised him that he would not return, not as he is now, carrying with him—poised for release and constant replay—all the sensations of one Lois Kramer. His victim. There are some urges Allie Pench will never (want to) feel again.

Nine girls await him: blue-kneed in micro-minis: gooseflesh, henna, velveteen. They greet him with a husky shout that makes him flinch. Bewildered, still unable to evict the stranger wholly from his mind, Allie stands frightened in their charge. He backs against the wet stone building, where they trap him. The first to reach him hurls herself headlong and seizes both his ears in red-nailed visegrips. Her kiss is open-mouthed; a lancing tongue pierces his surprise, then hands take his and guide them to the swell of tiny breasts.

Bile floods his throat, and hands begin again to cover his bare legs. The sequence starts again, and Allie Pench collapses to the street. Being raped. Again.

The girls shriek with delight as they run off through the drizzle, home to towels and hairdryers, and to phone calls where they all can share the game.

One man, a fragile fifty, hurries past. His head is locked. But his eyes dart left from time to time. He would like to say something to the man slowly climbing to his feet beside the R-R Center, to offer comfort. Of course he won't. It wouldn't be wise. Not on Second Friday.

sums

with John Jakes, first published in *Frights*, 1977

Two hundred yards off a country road, the Vineville School sits shielded from casual view by a screen of huge box elders, oaks, and sycamores. Between those trees and the road itself lies a swale of waist-high grass brushing whispers over the August noon. Two splintered posts, once whitewashed bright but long a faded dusty grey, stand sentinel in the grass to mark a narrow drive leading into the schoolyard. Its yellow width of sandy gravel has become a pair of dusty ruts in which the patches of wild rye, clumped clover gone to seed, and shoots of box elder all wave varieties of green. For years no one has entered the gravel drive. Few people travel over the country road, now that the interstate highway two miles south can speed the anxious through this idle countryside; and fewer still would think to glance aside, to waste a moment on the red brick building glimpsed by accident if at all.

But Harold Thorson knew the school was there. He knew every school in the country, the old, decayed, abandoned and the new alike. As county superintendent he knew them all in many ways. Each represented this or that bond issue, so much investment, so many staff and number of shouting, pushing children, maintenance costs and budgets, football schedules, lunchroom menus, heat and lights and chalk erasers. For all those schools, such factual matters lined themselves in ledgered rows in Harold's calculator mind. Only one of them stood out as different. Vineville. Where Thorson once had been among the children in the cloakroom frosty mornings, joking, teasing, hanging scarves and mittens on the numbered hooks and stamping snow from red galoshes as he fought with Bobby Reimer or the Kipness girl.

Thirty years ago. Before consolidation of the county schools, years before school buses and free lunch, when twice a month the children lined up giggling at Mrs. Baker's desk to get their goiter pills (lavender in color but chocolate on the tongue), before efficiency and ledgers and before the county board had modernized it all. And now, Vineville School—to be demolished in a month.

"Are you sure?" Harold asked them. "It's the last one in the county, maybe even in the state. Several people have proposed that we make a sort of museum of it, a place to house records or memorabilia." That last was a lie. Not several people at all. It was Harold's idea, but the board didn't need to know that.

For the next three or four minutes, the board members whispered among themselves. Nothing malicious, Harold knew. Just a little technique of theirs, a reminder that they owned the power; he held his position by the grace of their good will—that, and a slight majority vote.

Thickening heat pressed down on him. Bill Reimer's pipe lazed out ribbons of blue smoke. Harold wished they'd end the whispered conference. They all had other matters waiting. The Holcomb family's accusation, for one. To the effect that Mrs. Zarumian, Civics II, was a Marxist. "A Marxist!" God save us. Harold had an impulse to kill the Holcombs.

To spend his own life embroiled in such idle feints and parries... He supposed it served the youngsters in the long run. But it seemed so wasteful of the precious hours of a man's lifetime on earth. So useless, so incapable of adding up to anything worthwhile.

He tried to check his rising temper; his heart was hurrying in his chest, a three-legged colt cantering over gravel. Mental note. Back on the weight program. The doctor said—

"It's settled, Harold," Ellen Willets tapped her lacquered nails on the tabletop and glanced at the other Board members. They all nodded. Even Bill Reimer, lost in smoke.

Harold's breath stopped for a frightening instant. He crammed a hand into his coat pocket, reaching for the vial, one of the small white pills. His heart lumbered, his left upper arm ached. Budgets. Committee meetings. A Marxist—lord! For what? To what?

Fingers hidden in the pocket, curled around the vial—he could slip it out and take one of the pills in fifteen minutes, at their break—he said, "Bill? You remember. When we were both in Mrs. Baker's class? Don't you think..."

Reimer shook his head. "Tear it down."

Harold parked his three-year-old Chevy on the shoulder and walked across the softening blacktop to the faded driveway posts. That's what they all wanted. What could he do about it? What did he *want* to do about it? He had agreed, concealing his reluctance. And then, only this morning, walking the empty tiled and echoing hallways of the new high school, he had felt the impulse to come back to Vineville, for one last look.

The heat struck his body as a force. It accentuated the feel of extra pounds hanging on him like a laden yoke, pounds that intensified the heart problem about which he'd been repeatedly warned. Take it easy, Harold. Don't carry it all on your shoulders, Harold. But if he didn't deal with idiots like the Holcombs, who else would?

He tried to forget them, and the heat. But his upper left arm was throbbing again. He slipped a pill from the vial and tucked it under his tongue, anticipating the burn. Then he scuffed his oxfords in the dusty drive. The nitro helped. The memories flooded in on him.

Another August, thirty years before, he had ridden his bike two miles from home to wander the empty schoolyard the week before classes began. The months of that year, and of the years that followed, seemed a blur to him now, with only a few episodes standing bright and clear before him. The early September days, buttery at the morning edges as he walked to school. In the schoolyard, grasshoppers whirring up from cover at his feet—quick, fluttered explosions of sound that faded softly away. You caught them and said, "Spit and I'll let you go." There was recess, and the fort they'd built of planks and oil cans in the corner of the yard against Schmidt's fence. Eating a warm orange and folding waxed paper carefully to take it home for one more day, one more lunch. And Mrs. Baker.

He reached the treeline and took off his suit coat to sling it over his shoulder. The breeze cooled his sweat-soaked shirt and he felt loose, young again. To his right lay the playground area—no blacktop and expensive gym equipment in those days, only the ragged baseball diamond, each base a dusty gouge that filled with puddles in the late fall rain.

The school itself was smaller than he'd remembered, the bricks not so red, the steps not so tall. Plywood squares covered the windows like pennies on a deadman's eyes, but by squinting Harold could pretend he didn't see them. A squint. That's all it took. And the building, playground, all grew new again. He stood at the foot of the steps and turned his back to the school, surveying the playground. It really hadn't changed all that much, he hadn't changed all that much.

Then, to his right, he saw the clump of lilacs, spindly reeds grown tall and leafless near the base. It was his special place—had been his special place. A circle of bushes eight or more feet tall, their leaf-freighted tops bowed inward to create a canopy over the cool shaded spot. Where he'd often gone to eat his lunch, or tell the summer stories that all the children brought to Vineville in the fall.

Cool. And shaded. Beneath the overhanging bows the earth, nearly black and satin-like, felt smooth against his palms. Harold sat against the thickest clump of stalks and stared out through the mottled shadows at the school again. If he let his imagination play, he could almost hear the others—Billy Reimer and the Kipness girl, Dorcas Schmidt and all the rest—playing pom-pom-pullaway or prisoner's base in the hot sunlight while he lay in the pleasant shadow and observed. He felt the coolness of the earth, smelled orange peel and tasted peanut butter, heard the teeter-totter creak its grating rhythms.

Harold's head came up. His eyes opened. He started to laugh, softly, then checked it, embarrassed to make the sound with no one there to listen. He slid a foot back and pushed himself up. Bits of dying grass drifted from his trousers. The frozen sunburst of a burr slung to his cuff. He tasted the salt on his upper lip, tried to reconstruct. He remembered sitting down in the lilac clump. He didn't remember falling asleep.

His watch, and the disc of the sun, showed him he hadn't dropped off for long. He bent and pushed his way out of the lilacs. Though pleasant as a sentimental exercise, his return to Vineville now struck him as foolish. If he had hoped to find some clever answer to the problem of demolishing the place—or even an answer to the troubling question of why he was concerned at all—he hadn't. Moving with purpose over the shimmering playground, he was pleased that no one watched him, had been watching him return to his special place. These days there was no room for special places, and little understanding of the need for them. One schoolroom, one physical plant—one life—had to resemble the next. His included.

He hurried, conscious of the searing heat of the blacktop through the soles of his oxfords. A two-thirty meeting with the chairmen of the junior high science department. To discuss—what? The sun had addled him; he shook his head.

Yes. Centralized purchasing of lab supplies. Put your mind back on it, Harold. There was no way on God's earth to perpetuate his whim, to preserve Vineville School—nor any good reason why he should try.

He remembered dropping his coat on the concrete steps. The coat was gone.

Angry with himself—forgetting things already, Harold, sure sign of old age—he stalked back to the Chevy. Though the windows were down, the inside was an inferno. And empty. No coat.

Slowly, beginning to understand even then, he turned. He squinted through the filmy summer blaze, to the school door between the plywood squares which seemed to stare back at him. Take a step or two, closer—

He saw the vertical strip of blackness, wafer-thin but unmistakable. The door no longer touched the doorframe.

Without even asking the question, he believed he knew who had opened it. There was fear in his knowledge, but of a strange, almost relaxing quality. He started walking up the drive again, his chest tightening across its entire width.

He seldom allowed himself to think of that particular series of memories. Only when he'd had a beer or two, or when some reminiscent scent caught him off guard, did he invite those recollections back from where they lay hidden. They made smiling easier, at certain times. He didn't consider the memories now, either. But they lay inside him, bright as images on the videotape monitors all new high schools had to have—and his stomach hurt with excitement, anticipation.

Climb the stairs, not quickly, in fear, but with awful expectation. Awful, in the original meaning of it—

His freckled hand barely touched the green corroded handle. The door swung in. He smelled hot dust and animal droppings; saw the metal-framed desks, four rows creating aisles which narrowed into distant darkness. He pushed the door back. His throat felt thick. He moved from light to the inner shadows, expecting cruel heat. Perhaps the heat was there, and he was so cold he couldn't feel it.

Several plywood battens on the side windows hung agape, no longer a tight fit. Shafts of light penetrated, enough to show him his coat, resting across the top of a desk someone had dusted. The coat was carefully folded. Then in dappled shadow he saw Mrs. Baker, waiting.

He turned once. Out the door he saw the flare of sun on the Chevy's hood. And, distantly, the span of expressway, a diameter across the world, a disconnected span beginning nowhere, ending nowhere, yet endlessly busy—

When he turned back, Mrs. Baker was still there.

She smiled at him. "Hello, Harold. Won't you sit down?"

He squeezed into a front desk, not caring about the years of accumulated dirt that smeared his trousers. "I—I've never seen you here before."

"But I've seen you, when you came to remember. I thought the time had come to speak to you."

Mrs. Baker rose from her chair. She wore the outfit he remembered: a skirt, sweater, plain shoes. A gold heart locket on a chain of tiny links, the heart lying there between her breasts, where he'd so often stared at it, with longing. And with shame.

Mrs. Baker's sweater looked warm. Her forehead did not. Cool and curved as he remembered, it rose to the sweep of her fair hair. He had never gotten used to her name. A girl . . . Woman? What was she? Twenty-four, that much had been certain; twenty-four when he last saw her. He had never gotten used to her being *Mrs.* Baker. And now she still wore the cheap silver band on her left hand.

Harold had seen Mr. Baker from across the street as he emerged from Silbey Brothers' Funeral Home, at the end of that week in July when it had rained without stopping. Mr. Baker hadn't looked old enough to be studying for a graduate degree in engineering at State. But then, Mrs. Baker had never looked old enough to be a teacher, though she was two years out of Normal, and driving to State every day that summer for advanced work. On a Tuesday morning their used Hudson blew a tire on a rain-slick curve—

Damn him for not getting her a good car! Harold thought. Then he felt foolish, foolish as he felt, at times, among his memories. A rational corner of his mind kept reminding him: he hadn't looked old enough, back then, to care about a girl—a woman—a *Mrs.* Baker—twice his age. But then there was no explaining how you were marked in the yesterdays.

"I never knew how you felt till afterward, Harold," Mrs. Baker said. "I've never had the chance to tell you . . . I didn't want to frighten you—I hope you're not afraid now, but . . . It touched me a lot. It really did. I've wanted to take your hand and make you feel how much."

Harold wiped the back of his hand across his mouth. He noticed the top of the desk, now partially hidden by Mrs. Baker. *Mrs.* It still sounded wrong to him. Her fingers had been resting on the desk when he groped his way in. No marks disturbed the dust.

"You've watched me before?"

"Yes, whenever you've come. It's nice to have someone come back. No one else does."

"How long have you been here?"

"Actually, ever since the accident. What you see of me can't leave. A person's always a part of where they lived and breathed, you know. Perhaps they're never seen—or not often—afterward. But if they did more than just pass through a place, a part of them remains in it forever."

He lurched to his feet. "They're going to tear the school down. I'm the county school superintendent now—"

"I know, Harold. I have ways of keeping up."

"I can't stop it."

"That's why I knew I had to speak to you. You mustn't let them just destroy this place. It meant too much, to many people. And of course I'm being selfish. Once Vineville's gone, I don't know what will become of . . . this part of me."

"But why here?" Dust motes lifting on the slanted sunlight sparkled in the air between them. Harold squinted, leaned toward her. "You had another life, with . . . with *him*. Why here?"

"Now I know what really mattered." Her smile was warm, and real. It was! He knew that as he'd never known a thing before. "He and I were different, Harold. It took some time for me to see that. Even after—"

"He's married again, did you know?"

"It doesn't matter anymore. What matters is the present. We have to talk."

"Yes, Mrs. Baker." He sat again, folding his hands on the scarred desktop. One nervous finger traced initials carved and blackened in the polished wood.

She turned away, moving gracefully to the blackboard at the front of the room. "Arithmetic, Harold. Shall we work at numbers now?" Her smile drew a shy nod of response. "Good. You always enjoyed arithmetic, didn't you? I could see it in your eyes, the eagerness to move along, impatience with the others not so quick as you. Try this." She wrote on the black board: $12 + 30 =$

"Forty-two."

"And this." Again she wrote, the chalk whispering across the board, her wrist and arm an ivory blur before him. "Add this, Harold." $24 + 0 =$

"Twenty-four," he whispered.

"Aren't those numbers better?" She turned toward him slowly, her chin lifted high. "I waited for you, did you know? For all these years, each time I saw you passing by, the times you stopped and hesitated at the gate, and even when you thought of me and didn't know it, I was here. Waiting."

Without willing it, he was on his feet. "I have to tell you something." His voice was harsh, hoarse, and rasping. "Wait! There's something you don't know. I saw you and . . . you and *him*. I was outside your house one night, when . . . I couldn't help it, really! Walking past, and the shades were up, and . . ."

"I know." Gently she laid a hand on his cheek. "I knew at the time. It was you I was thinking of, only you. Even then, but what could I say? A boy half my age . . ." Her eyes were black and bottomless, her hand the scent of anise, sherry, tangerine.

"No!" He jerked away and stumbled clumsily against his desk. "Not yet." He sucked desperately at the fetid air. "Let me say it all. Those letters you got, *I* was the one who sent them. Vile! Terrible! How could I—"

"Not terrible, Harold. Pure, and lovely. You were only twelve, how else could you express what you felt? There's nothing to forgive, except your shyness, and the time you've made me wait." Again she reached to touch him.

Something flickered in the darkness to his left. He pulled away and peered into the haze-filled corners of the room. Nothing there. No one. As his eyes returned to hers it came again—a flash of light, a winking glitter. He ignored it. Her hands lay cool upon his cheeks and pulled him nearer, closer, toward her. The husky taste of copper filled his throat and made each breath a labor both of pain and promise. Through misted eyes he watched his own hands rise to rest upon her shoulders. Bare. Cream and honey to the touch, her sweater gone as easily as that. He ran a thumb along the straps which drew depressions in the softness of her flesh, and they were gone. Slowly his hands drifted down her back and traced the velvet hollows of her.

Then her voice was in his ear, each sibilant a rush of ocean or the summer wind across a plain of wheat. "Talk to me, Harold," she whispered. "Tell me you won't let them kill me. Not again. Not another time. This is me, here. This is you and I, here. Say you'll save me, save us, say that we can always meet like this."

Something rustled in the darkness at his back.

"Please?" Her lips caressed his ear, his shudders made him draw her closer till his arms ached from the strain of trying not to crush the warmth he held, finally, after all this time, held in his own arms. "Please? They'll never know. No one comes here now but you. The road's abandoned, no one passes by. How would they know?"

"I can't. How could I explain?"

Then she was hands. The shirt slid from his trembling shoulders as he stood in anguish. To protect her—somehow. To keep this moment. There had to be a way. "But if they found out—"

"How could they, Harold? Blind and hurrying, all of them, all the time. That road out there, this building, these are us. Not them. Let them have their highways, all the furious treadmills that they travel like some mindless creatures, driven, blind."

Whispering. The rush of yellow winds across a swamp.

He flinched and turned to look. Her nails scored fire down

his back and then his ribs, traced circles on his chest. The snicker of a buckle, and his belt released to free him from the bind of clothing dropped in whispers to the floor. "Is someone . . .? Did I hear . . .?"

Then she was tongues.

His hands explored, caressed, and kneaded while he trembled gravid with his need for her. He blinked against the hint of movement on all sides but couldn't wrench his gaze away from haloed shining hair that bobbed enticement on his chest. Her head tilted back, and she was all abandon, waiting now for him to act.

He choked back arguments, denials. "I'll try. You know I'll try."

Damp clouds surrounded them.

"I will," he said. "I will." And bent to cover lips that held a crimson welcome for him and his years of misted recollection.

Giggling voices. Breath at the nape of his neck.

She drew him lower. Settling, floating, drifting down. The floor a bed of clover now and musk that welcomed him. There was satin, tulle, and corduroy beneath his hands, while metronomes of light began their pulsing beat. He held his breath and felt the tension drawing bands across his chest.

"Har-uld's got a gir-rul, "Har-uld's got a gir-rul, "Har-uld's got a gir-rul."

He lunged in panic. His feet slipped on the dung-littered floor and he crashed awkwardly to his knees.

"That will be enough of that, boys and girls."

Mrs. Baker stood over him, tapping one toe impatiently. She posed in anger with her arms folded, and the sweater hung from her shoulders fluttering in the wet winds that rushed through the room.

"Well, Harold? Are you going to lie there all day? Take your seat, please. And the rest of you, stop that noise this instant!"

He stood up, wondering if he resembled an old-time burlesque comic, the way he reached—no sense hesitating—and pulled up his trousers and buckled the belt. In the light-slants, Schmidt's thousand-dollars worth of wire and bands winked again before she covered her mouth. She couldn't cover her laugh.

"Harold? I'm waiting—"

"Ooo, Har-uld, she's waiting, better kiss her," Billy Reimer giggled.

Harold forced his eyes away from the shadow-children, their faces moving now and again as if created of smoke. Yet he recognized each one, and each detail: Billy Reimer's perpetual ink-stain, a shapeless smeared tattoo on the inner side of his right index finger; the puckered vertical scar on the chin of the Kipness girl where she'd caught a hard-hit baseball one recess.

"Harold?"

He let the near-reality around him darken, drifting, faded, until his eyes bore down a tunnel into her eyes. Amused eyes, but not unkind amusement. The sharing of private, feverish matters; matters for two, no less, no more. Her eyes changed then; he saw a coppery inquisitiveness. He looked past her to the board.

$12 + 30 =$

And back. *I'm waiting,* the eyes said.

"Let me go outside a minute," he told her.

"We know where you're go-ing," Billy Reimer began and was joined by chanters: "We know where you're go-ing—"

He tried to speak to her without words. She understood

and nodded. "It will be time for the dismissal bell soon. Class, stop that silly singsong. Open your social studies book to the section we were studying yesterday. As you'll remember, we were talking about natural resources..."

He turned and stumbled up the dung-pelleted aisle, his coat over his arm. He closed the door behind him and sat on the concrete steps, blasted by the day's open furnace. The pain in his left upper arm increased, his heartbeat seemed quicker, the thrilling flutter of a trapped sparrow. He breathed with difficulty.

He fished out a second pill—the maximum he was allowed in eight hours—and this time he chewed and swallowed it, blinking away sweat from his eyelashes.

Across the distance, the blurred span of the superhighway began and ended in unknown places. He half-heard its repetitive hum. He thought of the annual budget, of crying pregnant girls, playground fights, coaches struggling for their livelihood—

One of them, Wodmer, a heap of debts and a record of 0-19 for his basketball team, had done it, finally, inside his thirty-six payment station wagon, with a vacuum cleaner hose through the window. And only six hours after Harold had bought him a beer, trying to convince him that there were other positions; that, with his influence, he might be able to ask for reinstatement, though of course he had no hope of it. Two influential board members wanted a new coach, and that was that. So much motion. Waste motion. Like the endless heat-snake that sped along the distant superhighway.

He sat a long while, adding it up. He wasn't happy with the total, but at least the process of calculation enabled him to reach a decision.

How difficult would it be? He was surprised that it was no more difficult than reaching out to pick up a drink of cool water. He simply—decided.

At once, the heat began to bother him less, his left upper arm stopped aching. His heart no longer clattered within his chest; he couldn't even feel it.

Was it all that easy?

Apparently.

He hunched back in what little shade the eaves provided. He closed his eyes, feeling both a little sad and certain that he'd done the right thing. It was best this way, as well as irrevocable.

Then a jingling inside the school—her hand-bell—brought a scurry and the treble drone of voices. He stood. His body felt light, virtually weightless. He positioned himself beside the door, waiting for them to come out.

The door didn't open, but all at once, on the steps beside him, he glimpsed a bandaged kneecap, a merry eye, a winking upper brace, and freckles, the children insubstantial as autumn leafsmoke. Their voices grew indistinct as they ran off around the corner of the school house, on up the dusty road—homeward. He couldn't see them clearly in the day's simmering blaze, and yet he could. He relished watching them run, carefree, unburdened.

Only when the sound of nearby crickets humming in the weeds had covered their fading voices, when the children were finally gone, did he turn to enter. He found it no longer necessary to operate the handle of the door. That amused him, somehow.

"Look, I've been thinking about you—"

"I'm glad you have, Harold. Have you decided? Can you stop them from destroying this place?"

"There's no way. It's too late, even if I wanted to try. You see, something changed while I was thinking out there. That is, I changed. At least I think I did—I wanted to, decided to. One of the reasons I did was because I knew there's no way on God's earth to stop them from tearing down the school. What I'm saying to you is, we'll have to go from here. Leave before they kill this building, and us in it. That way, we can at least be together..."

The drowning, beautiful eyes swallowed him in their wonder: "You don't want to go back? To come join me?"

"The thing is, I can't—anymore."

He extended his hand for her to touch. It was a different touch than when he'd held her only moments earlier; unreal, yet much fuller of sensation—like and like caressing."

"Harold, kiss me."

"Can we—?"

"Harold, make love to me."

"Is it possible? I mean, the way we both are—?"

"We're the same now. If we can't make love..." The fire in her eyes bloomed like embers suddenly blown. She laughed. "If we can't, you certainly made a bad decision. Harold, I'm only teasing. If you couldn't stop Vineville coming down, why, yes. We'll take our chances—one and one."

"I honestly don't feel bad about it," he said, walking past her, his eye on the board. "Not a single regret. At least so far."

"I'll try to keep you in that frame of mind."

With sudden insight, clear and sharp, he sensed another change—he now guiding her—and smiled. "I just added it all up, and it came to—to a hell of a lot of wasted time." Chalk in his fingers. "This way, I'll have something." He erased the equal sign following "12 + 30," added a plus, a zero, an equal sign, then two numerals. He stepped back, pleased, and proud, the equation now correct.

12 + 30 + 0 = 42

He turned, dropped the chalk into the darkness, aware in passing that he never heard it strike the floor as his arms reached for her.

They watched from a distance, a distance measureable in many ways, as two sedans pulled into the dusty drive later that night. Roof lights whipped red swirls across the weed tops.

Then the ambulance came, and a towtruck for Harold's Chevy. He wasn't able to get a close look at the shape beneath the stretcher sheet. Two young kids loaded the stretcher at the school steps, but because of the darkness Harold couldn't be certain whether they were loading something, or nothing. They certainly weren't loading him; that is, any of him that mattered.

When the last state police cruiser raked its front wheels noisily onto the country road and disappeared behind the silent ambulance, Harold felt a little regret. But not much. He turned his back on the diminishing cruiser; in the turning, his eyes drifted past the span of superhighway. At night it was distinct: a hard black swath through the night, marked with dotted patterns—red beads strung one direction, white the other.

Harold smiled and said Mrs. Baker's first name aloud. Aloud, to them. He drew her down in the privacy of the lilacs.

Re-porter

first published in *TRACKS*, Fall–Spring 1977

The reporter's wife divorced him. He recorded impressions of the courtroom, interviewed attorneys and spectators, and noted on his stenopad four names-and-addresses as well as the time of day and room temperature. Three pages into his stenopad he looked up to discover the courtroom empty and the lights gone dark.

He waited two hours for the court clerk to recast the trial transcript in English. A copy cost him $28. It contained nothing useable.

He filed the story, knowing it would be cut to a two-inch column filler. His name and hotel address appeared in the second sentence. As plaintiff, his ex deserved pride of place in the lead. A sexist but traditional format.

He returned to his hotel and—after three mistakes–found his own room. Furniture offered no clue. The fox-hunt print hanging askew over the bed's headboard seemed to skip ahead of him from one room to the next. His red sock ID-ed his room. It lay on the floor beside the greasy-armed overstuffed chair near the window. The other three rooms he'd tried were sockless.

A 1999 Buick Skylark climbed the sidewalk at 42nd and Howard and pinned a woman against a liquor store. Helen Bart, age 27, of 6492 E. Royal Street, was pronounced dead on arrival at County General Hospital. She is survived by everyone reading about her death.

The reporter sharpened four pencils with a pearl-handled pocketknife.

His red felt-tipped pen circled several items in the late edition. All of them his, without bylines.

Merle Joiner of 6492 Carleton Place was featured in six of the items: divorced; winner of the New Mexico lottery; captured at the site of a whip-and-leather boutique he had terrorized for fifty-two minutes with a cleaver and mail-order can of Mace; arrested inside his crumpled 1999 Buick Skylark; promoted to Patrolman First Class for his single-handed capture of the man terrorizing a whip-and-leather boutique; and victorious in his suit against the estate of Helen Bart, whose occiput and gluteus had impacted with and shattered a $240 plate glass door of the liquor store Joiner owns.

Henry David Thoreau stopped reading newspapers. Long after he stopped buying newspapers. Soon after he stopped borrowing newspapers.

The reporter reviewed his book review. "Yesbut," it read. "While A . . . nevertheless B." "Unique among but comparable to . . ." His red felt-tipped pen deleted "Unique." His pencil replaced it with "Rare." @ $35 each, book reviews are the annuity that buys Monday-to-Friday's beer and Saturday's scotch.

The review was scheduled to run again Sunday, if the Book Editor received another book before Saturday noon. The Sunday edition requires 6-8 hours in composing. Ads first.

The book review (inserted last: a buffer) requires liminal attention.

The reporter worked on his acceptance speech for the Pulitzer Prize. In case.

He had in his hotel room sixty-two filled stenopads he could no longer read. Sixty-two pads, forty pages each. Sharp pencil points had torn through the top sheet. By page nine (unnumbered) the carbon marks grew faint. Pages 10-40 showed increasingly decreasing degrees of impression.

At his next divorce he saved $28 by making his own transcript of Helen Bart's complaints about his irregular habits and persistent demands upon her physical person. "Insatiable," he noted.

"Kind of boring," is what she said.

It's good to get quotes whenever possible. (One aging copy-editor demands "quotation" as the noun form, but the slot-man tends not to pass him copy containing "quote.")

William Randolph Hearst queried Richard Harding Davis: "What are the news?" From Cuba, Davis answered: "Not a new."

In the Public Library Reading Room three men wearing a total of seven sweaters (five cardigan, two pullover) rustle through back issues. Fungus on the brittle yellowed pages infects their sclerotic fingers with mild neural dermatitis. Each man has ink stains on his thumb. Each marks his place on the wooden bench with a thumbprint. Leaving the wooden bench in a sudden lunge for the foreign editions newly hung on split bamboo display poles, each slides serge over and erases the thumbprints. They return to quarrel about domain.

Re-porter

The reporter bought his scotch at Merle Joiner's liquor store. He admired Joiner's new plate glass door and jotted down details. Width, 32 inches; height, 84 inches, "Owens-Corning" graven on the lower right (inside) corner (lower left) outside (corner).

His red felt-tipped pen struck out a forgotten name from an earlier item recording someone's divorce proceedings. His pencil inserted the name Merle Joiner.

At the Public Library he took from his leftleg pocket his human-interest story. He sharpened his red felt-tipped pen with the pearl-handled knife. He counted the sweaters and the men. One of them was reading an item the reporter thought he might have written. The missing byline was familiar and quite possibly his. He grew proud and considered his Pulitzer Prizes.

One old man ate the sports page and stood on the serge-smeared thumbprints to recite the scores.

The reporter found that humanly interesting.

Ninety-seven newspapers in the Knight chain cancel Jeanne Dixon's column, as she had predicted they would.

The reporter has an office at the newspaper. He shares it with sixteen others who type with knit typewriter cozies dropped over their copy to prevent plagiarism by the incompetent seated beside each of them . . . moving North to East. (N.E.W.S. is a compass-face gone Moebius.) The reporter sits in the exact center. His typewriter is an IBM Mag-Card II. Yes, typewriter. Word processors are reserved for byline columnists in the carpeted office. He pushes a button and flips a switch and the Mag-Card II types his story.

Rookie reporters type their story manually. Many are still

only porters, promotions pending. Most have fewer than sixty-two stenopads stored in their homes or hotel rooms. Some have yet to acquire pencils to sharpen and write only with red felt-tipped pens.

The reporter feels superior to them, though inferior to columnists (even columnists without their airbrushed photos atop the text).

Helen Bart is Society Editor.

The composing room is in Lagado. A block of cross-grained oak with the generic address on it is fixed to the press. Four digits, randomly selected: 6492.

Helen Bart of 6492 and Merle Joiner of 6492 will marry Sunday. Divorce Monday. Kill Tuesday. Die Wednesday.

The reporter has a four-day week.

Charlie Brown matures and presides at the wedding of Brenda Starr and Beetle Bailey held at the homes of Novak and Evans at 6492 and 6492.

THE TIMES swells to four crossword puzzles each edition. No one notices them, printed horizontally across the raw edges of 118 pages of B. Altman ads.

Woodward Redford and Dustin Bernstein have gold-plated stenopads. Platinum-filled Eversharp mechanical pencils provided for promotional considerations. Personalized red felt-tipped Cross pens. Sixty-three stenopads (sixty-two of them dummies) in their home(s).

The reporter vacates his hotel room and moves into his office. His typewriter is the IBM Mag-Card II with the red sock atop it. He smears an inky thumbprint on the typewriter on-off switch.

The news buzzes electronically webward, no longer printed

on paper. Reporters listen to one another's typewriters/ printers clattering out the ~~day's week's month's annual~~ story and watch it flash screen-to-screen.

The reporter is divorced. No one in the courtroom takes notice. With his pearl-handled knife he carves the details in Helen Bart of 6492. . . .

Take a Number

first published in *TRACKS*, Spring 1979

Born 4:17 a.m. February 29th, in the year of his life zero . . . Anthony Emerson.

Born, then 4 decades of the uneventful, with occasional moments of pleasure: the surprise of his first lamb curry; Bach in stereo while he soaked in his wife's bubble bath; his 2nd sexual encounter (the 1st met with *interruptus* when a policeman's flashlight swept shriveling terror over Young Tony and Allegra Kleinschmidt in the back seat of her '97 Plymouth).

Less frequently he felt pain: broken arm; promotion denied; the moment a beautiful 21-year-old called him "sir" and meant it. No spectacularities about it, his life was all of a mundane piece.

On his 41st birthday he returned home from work to 3 greetings. 1 expected, 1 monthly, 1 crucial. Bette had made him the usual chocolate carrot cake. It stood cooling on the kitchen counter. He sidestepped around Karen's tricycle into the dining room. On the table lay the mail: a circular from Kleins, a postcard from the Winklers flaunting their Jamaica vacation in crowing ball-point scrawl, and 11 bills. He counted them, unopened.

Karen in clogs came clattering down the stairs, crying. "Mommy told me. Mommy said you're *old!*" Blue-black hands. She'd been at the carbon paper again.

"Is that how you welcome the birthday boy?" He snatched her up in the whirl of their nightly greeting, counting her ribs for the giggle it always earned.

Not this time. "40 is *old*," Karen said. "Mommy told me."

She probably had. Not cruelly, of course, but in her matter-of-fact, it's time-you-knew-the-facts-young-lady voice. Mommy was 28, evidence—Anthony's neighbors claimed with some lecherous envy at the thought of bedding taut-thighed Bette Emerson—of Anthony's blooming late. "You smart bugger. No guy should get married before 35," Al Winkler told him across their common privet hedge, side-slipping through to grow heavy-eyed confidential. "By then he knows what he's getting into. Hey? Hey?" An elbow in the ribs.

"Mommy's right about 40, but I'm only 39. When I hit 40, I turned around and started back the other way."

"Really?" Her pouting lip begged persuasion. "You have wrinkles." She smeared carbon blacking on his cheek, her hand warm.

"Daddies don't lie. I'm 39, next year I'll be 38, and so on."

"When will I be 38?"

Well, let's see. You're 20 now—"

"*Daddy!*" with a giggle. "I'm 5 ½."

"Okay, 5 ½. That means when I'm 38 you'll be 6 ½. When I'm 37 you'll be 7 ½. When I'm 37, you'll be 7. And—"kissing her nose, her smile for reward"—and I'll meet you! We'll both be 23 the same year. How's that?"

Not a very original argument. But then, for 41/39 years Anthony Emerson had straddled or circled the mean. Never an exact "average"—certainly no statistically-central freak of perfect conformity—he seldom swung to extremes. His life ranged the gamut from J to N.

Or it had, till this prime nexus, when he fluked his way into a miracle. On his 41st/39th birthday, himself a 2/29 baby, pledging to meet a 5-year-old on their common 23rd birthday, 11 bills in his (left) hand . . . he spoke what he considered folly, and the echo of his comment touched the Universal Axis.

A tremor in eternity.

An engineer atop a promontory watched obliteration. A honeycomb concrete dam, pride of his career, burst like a squashed clam under the pressure of millions of tons of sludge-laden water that boiled irresistibly down a narrow valley and jumbled a 419-home subdivision like so many strawberry boxes, while the engineer glared at his slide rule and muttered, "That damn decimal point."

Anthony Emerson's 67 gray hairs went auburn. Again. His new Dockers grew loose at the waist and his shirt collars tightened around the firming neck muscles earlier gone slack during the ascending march of birthdays past. He was well into countdown, 34 and counting, before he knew certainly that he'd conquered the numbers.

Oh, he'd had indications. Past 6 months pregnant on Anthony's 41st/39th birthday,

Bette was still pregnant. For a year or 2 it had intrigued or puzzled the few doctors who bothered to believe Bette's claim. By now the novelty was gone. Bette was content. The fetus pulsed normally. Her condition affected their lives only on anniversaries when Anthony wished he could dance closer to her. But that was all. They were a 21st century statistically perfect American family: 1.7 children.

Through an accident of will, he was Chronos.

And having met with success unexpected in common hours, Anthony took to cooking the numbers intentionally. He began timidly enough. A $1.29 bottle of yellow enamel and a #2 camel's-hair brush changed the 3 on his license plate to an 8. The parking tickets he accumulated papered the inside of his toolkit.

His work at The Bullens Company was exemplary. His subordinates mistook his younging for aging gracefully, and his superiors made him troubleshooter for the entire plant, a step that led him 1 day into the bowels of the stamping room.

whipsnicker whipsnicker ta-clump ta-clump, thrussssh, 1 brown blucher shuffled downchute onto the conveyor belt, was spun into position, had the figures 14EE stamped on its imitation composition lining; and the shoe slid with its mate into a Bullens Company box.

Experimenting, Anthony removed a single ratchet from the stamping wheel. Random became the rule, paired bluchers stamped 8C and 12D or 7 1/2EE and 9B, perfect pairs all, imperfectly labeled.

No 1 noticed.

He smiled and for months watched sales figures dot-dash a horizontal across the graph. No 1 complained about misnumeraled goods except Christine Schlager in Pewaukee, Wisconsin, who returned a single mangled Cuban-heel pump with an angry letter describing the pain suffered by her Dachsund in trying to assuage his 7AA hunger with a 9C ("and I never wore a 9 in my life!")

Once a statistician drowned while wading across a stream that had an average depth of 3 feet. Once is enough.

Less original than he considered himself, Anthony Emerson nevertheless outstripped his more imaginative but less committed colleagues in the war against numbers . . . or against those for whom numerals are numbers.

He learned the Master Identifying Number of the Literary Guild's computer bank and under that number joined the Book-of-the-Month Club *for* the Literary Guild. The Guild never rejected a monthly offering and never paid for any selections received. (Historians recall the Battle of Camp Hill PA and the blue lightning clash of computers in the crater that stands a perpetually smoking admonition to those who would ignore *THE*4TH*NOTICE*.)

Ever faster Anthony Emerson attacked. As he grew younger, his power grew more awesome, unknown to all but him and The Universal Bookkeeper ("b OO KK EE per": 3 consecutive double letters, unique in English, mysterious in triunity).

He and his wife phoned Karen in college. Often. When their telephone bill matched the GNP of Chad, AT&T/Bell/McSprint limited them to calls lasting 6 minutes or $60, whichever came first. Anthony retaliated. He direct-dialed Seattle on a (Tele-Bargain) Sunday: access number, area code, exchange, 4 digits of the 5. He didn't dial the final 7. (He didn't dial a final anynumber, but 7 was the 1 he'd had in mind.)

In scant moments the unused 7 disappeared from all phone dials and punch-pads within the continental U.S.

Take a Number

In hours AT&T/Bell/McSprint forgot even the shape of the numeral formerly snuggled beside PRS on the dial.

In days the number seven followed the numeral 7 into oblivion. Other numbers shifted downscale to fill the gap. With Pi now 7-less, all circles grew elliptical.

Grammarian's riddle: which is better, 2+5 IS 8, or 2+5 ARE 8?

Eight bits make a byte. And a dollar.

On yet another anniversary young Tony Emerson and gray-haired Bette ("fetchingly enceinte in yellow tulle," burbled one spinster neighbor to another over the gossip hotline) danced the night away. Tony paid the dinner check in cash, charging on his Diners Club card only the tip.

Driving home on the tollway he tossed 4 quarters into the conical tollgate basket in the Exact Change lane. The first (and required) quarter raised the toll barrier arm in a 90 degree counterclockwise arc, allowing Anthony through.

The other 3 quarters bought an additional counterclockwise arc of 270 degrees that impacted the next vehicle in line. The barrier arm stopped only after it completed the circle, sliced a slit in the macadam roadbed and upward into the cab of Roy Barrett's Heinekens delivery truck through the running board, frame members, floorboard, seat braces, springs and padding to within 3 centimeters of the worst goosing of Barrett's life.

Hippity hoppity
Anthony Emerson

Stepped on a knifeblade while
Running a race.

Though not the winner he
Finished the course with his
Sesquipedalian
Hobbling pace.

At age 10, Tony Emerson buried his aged wife, said farewell to his 12-year-old grandson, and set out to do serious battle.

"Let him go," Karen told her son. "When a man gets to 70 he's allowed to have crochets. It's grief, is all. You know, 'cause Grandma died."

He bought Sears-Montgomery to their knees by returning to their stores items charged at Ben Franklin and having unwarrranted refunds credited to his (never-used) S-M charge account. He later paid Ben Franklin with Sears-Montgomery stock certificates he found cluttering his new office after the takeover.

As the first CEO of Emerson-Sears-Montgomery he had access to invisible ink (catalog p. 347, "discontinued"). That was the point of the takeover. What did he want with a corporation that kept its books with numerals?

On bank deposit slips Anthony printed his own account number, invisible to the eye but not to the electronic sorting equipment that had replaced judgment in every major financial institution outside of Georgia's Lance National Bank. He left the invisibly pre-printed slips beside the ill-functioning ballpoint pens on every counter of every bank in NYC. Other depositors penned in their own account numbers, never seen by human eye as the electronic sorter did its (or actually Anthony's) task.

A month later, in 1 transaction he withdrew from his account all the money/numerals in North America.

He bought—and shut down—the Social Security Administration, revenge for their having denied him an unlisted numeral.

Long after we all became nameless numbers in the Grand Bank in D.C., boy met girl in a bar. They shared drinks and body brushings: knee against knee, breast against shoulder. He asked her name. "7215509. And yours?" "6346065." "That's funny," she said. "You don't look Jewish."

Only the IRS stood between Little Tony and pristine numberlessness. For a time. Till he was summoned for an audit. The large magnet he slipped behind the cabinet of the spinning masterdrum reduced all IRS records to 86 miles of virginal, Mylar-coated ribbon and their ZIP-disc backups into 62 etching-erased DVD frisbees.

Abacuses became the rage.

Tiny Tony never consummated his courtship of the Hong Kong abacus cartel. Coitus near, he reached instead his 0th birthday. Chuckling in wonder, he was unborn at 4:17 A.M., February 29th, in the year of his life, Zero, a phenomenon misunderstood by mourners at the interment of a sclerotic husk once named Anthony Emerson.

It really happened that way. He did go back. You can reverse the numbers, or deny them, or erase them. Not original at all, Anthony Emerson. Before him, after him, simultaneous with his chance discovery, 468,911 others had found/will find/are finding similar paths. Each goes unnoticed but for a momentary twitch of the Universal Axis.

It really happened that way, in an instant, in the pulseblink touch of his daughter's grimy hand upon his cheek.

Take a number.

Richard E. Peck, 2012

Vintage Richard E. Peck, 1972
Photo by Townsend Wentz.

In the '60s, Richard E Peck began writing newspaper columns (later collected in *Passing Through* and *Traveling at My Desk*) and Science Fiction. You're holding the earliest examples of his SF. Both apprenticeships led to his subsequent published work, a dozen produced plays, two industrial films, two network TV shows, numerous scholarly articles, a golf book, and seven novels--most recently *Schmidt's Mill*. He now enjoys writing—two books a year is the goal—and frequent speaking to social clubs and corporations.

Contact him at www.richardepeck.com.

CPSIA information can be obtained at www.ICGtesting.com
Printed in the USA
LVOW040644071112

306214LV00002B/4/P